Now was the time to tell Dylan that Bryce hadn't sent her and that no one was ever going to mistake her for a NASCAR driver's girlfriend.

But suddenly the thought of slogging through dinner alone while newly engaged Marvin and Penelope canoodled in some dark corner was simply too pathetic.

The NASCAR driver standing in front of her at this very minute believed she could pass as his girlfriend. Why on earth couldn't she see what that would be like?

What if she showed up at her actuarial banquet with this walking shrine to testosterone? Wouldn't that show Marvin—and everyone?

She had no purse, no room key, nothing. Not so much as a tissue. She'd never done anything this wild in her life, until now.

Oh, and it felt good.

Dear Reader,

We novelists tend to live in our heads. We dream up characters and they say, do and appear exactly as we want them to. So there I was, merrily writing *Speed Dating* with its fictitious cast when I got a call from my editor Marsha Zinberg giving me the opportunity to have NASCAR driver Carl Edwards appear in my book. After the screams of excitement died down, I realized that I had a challenge ahead of me. This was a real live person and he was going to be in my book, interacting with my imaginary friends—ah, I mean, my characters.

What followed was one of the most enjoyable experiences of my career. I had a chance to meet and interview Carl (and he is absolutely as gorgeous and nice as he appears), I toured Rousch Racing and watched these cars being built. I met some fans, and toured the track at Charlotte.

I'm indebted to Melissa Gawalko and Michelle Renaud from Harlequin Books for making that trip so much fun, to Catherine McNeill of NASCAR and to Matthew Braydich of Rousch Racing for all the help.

Most of all, of course, I'm indebted to Carl Edwards, who, in my humble opinion, makes a pretty good romance hero.

Speed Dating has been a fun and crazy ride, and I hope you enjoy it as much as I have. Please stop by and visit me on the Web for more at www.nancywarren.net.

Happy reading,

Nancy

NASCAR

SPEED DATING

Nancy Warren

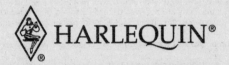

HARLEQUIN®

TORONTO • NEW YORK • LONDON
AMSTERDAM • PARIS • SYDNEY • HAMBURG
STOCKHOLM • ATHENS • TOKYO • MILAN • MADRID
PRAGUE • WARSAW • BUDAPEST • AUCKLAND

ISBN-13: 978-0-373-21769-4
ISBN-10: 0-373-21769-2

SPEED DATING

Copyright © 2007 by Harlequin Books S.A.

Nancy Warren is acknowledged as the author of this work.

NASCAR® and the NASCAR Library Collection are registered trademarks of the National Association for Stock Car Auto Racing, Inc.

This edition published by arrangement with Harlequin Books S.A.

www.eHarlequin.com

Printed in U.S.A.

NANCY WARREN

Nancy Warren is a *USA TODAY* bestselling author of more than thirty romantic novels and novellas. She has won numerous awards for her writing and in 2004 was a double finalist for the prestigious RITA® Award. Nancy lives in the Pacific Northwest, where she includes among her hobbies a growing fixation with the NASCAR channel. For more on Nancy, her releases, writing tips and background visit her on the Web at www.nancywarren.net.

This book is dedicated to Marsha Zinberg,
an amazing editor and a delight to work with.
Thank you. And a big thank-you to my favorite
NASCAR driver, Carl Edwards, for being a wonderful
character and a good sport in every sense of the word.

CHAPTER ONE

KENDALL CLARKE was looking forward to the most exciting night of her life.

Only thirty-one years old, she would be the youngest recipient of the prestigious Sharpened Pencil Award for being chosen Actuary of the Year.

For the hundredth time, she tracked across the carpet of her hotel room in Charlotte, North Carolina, to practice the acceptance speech she'd give tonight at the closing banquet of the actuarial association dinner. She wanted to come across as humbled to be receiving this great honor, but also proud of the work done by her company.

"Ladies and gentleman, colleagues, friends." She paused as she'd been taught in the public speaking refresher course she'd taken the second she learned she'd be making this speech. *Breathe,* she reminded herself. *Look out at the audience. Smile.* "Trust is the cornerstone of our business," she informed the blue-upholstered chair in the corner of the room. She put an emphasis on *trust.* Such a nice, strong word to start a speech with. *Trust.*

There was an hour or so before she needed to head down to ballrooms A and B, where the American Association of Actuaries was holding its annual conference and awards banquet. She'd sent her dress down for pressing earlier in the day, wanting everything to be perfect. She bit her lip. The dress ought to be back.

Willing to leave nothing to chance, she called down to Housekeeping. After many a long, lonely ring of the phone, a hesitant female voice said, *"Hola?"*

It didn't take Kendall long to realize that the woman spoke almost no English, and Kendall's Spanish wasn't any better. She thought after a few minutes of labored conversation that she'd got her request through. She wanted them to hurry up with her dress and send it to her room.

She'd barely replaced the receiver in its cradle when it rang.

"Kendall Clarke," she said at her most formal, because you never knew at a business conference who might be calling. But, as she'd hoped, the voice at the other end belonged to Marvin Fulford, her colleague and fiancé.

"Kendall, it's me, Marvin," he said. He was so sweet. They never shared a room when traveling because both agreed it gave the wrong impression. Indeed, this time Marvin had gone so far as to book a room on a different floor.

"Hi, Marvin. Are you going to pick me up here so we can arrive at the banquet together?" That was one of the perks of working with your fiancé, she'd long thought. She rarely had to attend big business events alone.

"Um, I was hoping to come up now and talk to you for a few minutes."

He sounded odd. As if he was nervous. Probably on her behalf. "Great. I can practice my speech on a real person. Come right up."

Or maybe, she thought, as she replaced the phone, he wanted to make love before the ceremony. Her pulse quickened. What a wonderful way to relax before her big moment. Their sex life had been sparse to nonexistent lately, so the idea of him wanting to jump her bones right before the banquet filled her with delight.

She'd planned to surprise him with some sexy new lingerie she'd bought—well, sexy for her. Her makeup, hair and nails were all done, courtesy of the hotel salon, so it took her no time at all to slip into the black demi bra and high-cut panties and the black silk slip she'd bought at Victoria's Secret. Her black stockings were sheer as a whisper and her black sandals were strappy, with a low but shapely heel. She'd debated stilettos but you didn't work in the actuary business without learning a lot of very useful facts, like the stats on back pain and injury stemming from the wearing of high-heeled shoes. Besides, she didn't want to stumble on the way to the stage. Not in front of all her professional colleagues.

She was tingling with anticipation when a knock sounded on her door. Of course, they wouldn't have a lot of time, but with Marvin not a lot of time was necessary. Oh, well. Once they were married and things settled down, they could spend more time on the intimate part of their relationship.

She struck a sultry pose, then felt ridiculous, so she simply reminded herself to stand up straight, then opened the door.

Marvin stood on the other side wearing khakis and

a golf shirt. The fact that he wasn't yet dressed for the banquet made her very glad she'd slipped into her sexy underwear.

But Marvin didn't even seem to notice. He glanced up and down the hall before he entered her room, looking furtive and not remotely like a man bent on a prebanquet quickie.

"Marvin? Is everything all right?" She'd wondered if he was a little jealous that she'd received this honor instead of him. Surely he could be happy for her, as she'd have been for him. They were planning to spend their lives together. Wasn't a marriage all about mutual respect, compatibility and support?

"I have something to tell you, Kendall, that may shock you," he said, glancing up and then away. His pale blond hair was shorter than usual, she noted. He must have had a trim. He'd never be confused with Brad Pitt, but he was a pleasant-looking man, she thought. Maybe a little on the pale side, but he did suffer from asthma.

She smiled at him. "Is it good news?" This was the kind of conference where networking was abundant. Had he been offered a job of some kind?

"Good news?" He glanced at her again, as though surprised by the question. Then, as was typical of him, he took a moment to ponder. Marvin always looked at all sides of a question. It was a quality she admired in him.

"In some ways it is good news. Very good news," he said. "But *you* may not think so."

"It's a job offer, isn't it? Is it very far away from Portland?" The possibility had always existed that one of them would get a better offer elsewhere. They'd never discussed what they'd do in that eventuality. Did she have to be tested now? Couldn't Marvin have waited until after the banquet?

"No. It's not a job offer. It's…" He blew out a breath. "It's personal. I don't know how to begin."

The first icy claws of apprehension scratched the surface of her happiness. "Personal?"

"I never meant to hurt you, Kendall. I swear. The whole thing was…unplanned."

"What whole thing?" she asked, feeling a numbness start to creep into her toes.

Marvin's pale cheeks took on a faint pink hue and he looked everywhere but at her. She'd never seen him so uncomfortable.

"I've fallen in love," he said at last. "With someone else."

She blinked. Opened her mouth and then closed it again.

When she didn't speak, he went on. "I never meant for it to happen. To hurt you. Behind your back. I don't know what I was thinking. I wanted to tell you, but I didn't know how. I…"

"You're in love with someone else?" she repeated stupidly.

"Yes."

"But we've interviewed caterers, picked out china. We're on the third draft of our guest list…"

He was rubbing a spot on the carpet with the toe of his brown tasseled loafer, giving the nub of worsted his full attention. After she petered out, there was a moment of painful silence.

"Who is it? This person you've fallen in love with." Her voice was calm, for which she'd always be grateful.

"Penelope Varsan." He made eye contact and then his gaze slid away.

Kendall stared at him. "Our colleague? You've been seeing a woman we both work with behind my back?"

"It was an accident. I swear. We were both working late night after night on the Wayman file and…one thing led to another. I didn't know how to tell you. I'm sorry."

"Why are you telling me now?" She raised a hand to her head. "I can't even think. I'm supposed to give a speech and all I'll be able to concentrate on is that my date for the evening is in love with another woman."

"Well, um, that's why I wanted to tell you now. You see…" He sighed heavily and sat down in the wing chair beside the small table where she'd set up her laptop. "Penelope's going to have a child."

"She's pregnant?" Kendall's voice was barely a whisper.

"Yes."

"Then this must have been going on for months."

"About four months."

"Oh, Marvin. How could you betray me like that?"

"I wanted to wait until after this conference to tell you. You must have felt that things haven't been close between us for some time."

She snorted. "Now I know why."

"I like and respect you, Kendall. You have a fine mind and you're an excellent actuary. I mistook professional respect for…warmer feelings."

"What are you saying?" All her life she'd searched for the one person who would love her forever. A man like her father, who'd be faithful and true to his family. She wasn't looking for fireworks and matinee-idol, multimillionaire hotshots. All she'd ever wanted was a steady, decent man who'd love her and any family they might have. She'd aimed so low, and still she'd failed. Somehow she needed to understand why.

"You're a wonderful person, but you're not... Well, Penelope's exciting. She's passionate. I realized that's what was missing with us."

Her leaden stomach grew heavier. "So, I'm not exciting enough for you?"

"It's not your fault, Kendall. I need more."

"Well, I guess you're getting it." She rubbed her forehead. "I can't believe this."

"As you may know, when women are in a delicate situation, they can become quite emotional."

"Thank you for the prenatal lesson, Marvin."

"The thing is, Penelope's feeling very insecure and it's making her a bit clingy."

"What is your point?"

"She wants me to sit with her at the banquet tonight. That's why I had to tell you right away. I would, of course, have said no. I want to support you. This is a big night for you and for our firm, but she's carrying my child." He paused for a moment, and she could tell he was savoring the phrase. His narrow chest swelled a little. "I have to think of my family."

"So, you're dumping me. Just like that. Right before the biggest night of my life."

He smiled at her, obviously relieved to have the burden of his confession off his chest and no hysterics to wade through. "You're strong, Kendall. You don't need me the way Penelope does."

He walked to the door and opened it, then glanced

back. "Good luck tonight." He sounded as though he really meant it.

After the door shut behind her ex-fiancé, Kendall stood there feeling frozen and numb. Bits of thoughts and phrases were jumbled up in her head. *Not exciting enough. Pregnant. I need more.*

And through it all flickered the humiliating knowledge that this relationship had gone on for months under her nose and she'd never noticed. She had the sick feeling that she was the only one in the office who hadn't.

This was supposed to be the night of her greatest triumph, not her greatest humiliation.

If only she could think more clearly.

She stood there in her new underwear and slowly tugged the engagement ring off her finger and regarded the diamond solitaire. Like her dreams, it was modest.

She ought to return it to Marvin, but he was just thrifty enough that he might offer the ring to Penelope.

She put the ring on the dresser where it made a tiny click. She'd leave it as a tip for the maid.

Having decided the ring's future to her satisfaction, she glanced at her clock and discovered with horror that the banquet was starting in fifteen minutes. Luckily she was ready. No, wait, she wasn't. Something was missing. She looked around vaguely.

Oh, of course. Her dress. The one Marvin had helped her pick out at Nordstrom.

DYLAN HARGREAVE gave a rebel yell into the headset, knowing he'd half deafen his spotter and any of the crew who were listening.

"She's sweet," he yelled, feeling the grab of the tires,

the tightness of tail. He accelerated into Turn Three at the Speedway in Charlotte, pulling the wheel hard left, hanging on to control as he fought for more speed. A glance at the oversize tachometer told him the engine was cooperating.

Charlotte was his track. He always did well here. Being a North Carolina boy, it was important for him to place high in Sunday's race for a lot of reasons. Today's training run was feeling good. He was pumped; the team members were working together like magic.

The run of bad luck they'd suffered recently was about to end. He loved race week in Charlotte, culminating in the big race.

Sunday, he fully intended to take a victory lap.

He owned this course, and anybody who wanted to try and take him better be ready to do serious battle.

Then he felt the speed fall away as though somebody'd turned off the ignition.

"Aaaaw, no!" he yelled, as a multicolored blur of cars zoomed past him like a swarm of bees. It was only a practice to make sure everything was running smoothly, but it was clear that things on the Hargreave team weren't going smoothly at all.

After they'd towed the car into the huge garage, by the hauler that housed a second race car and all the tools and spare parts they might need, Mike Nugent, his crew chief, slapped him on the back. "Probably the fuel line, Dy. We'll get it fixed for Sunday."

Dylan nodded. He didn't bother saying anything. Every one of the glum faces on the team reflected his own expression. Luck. They really needed some luck.

Preferably the good kind.

As usual, even though it was only a practice, loads of fans were out, a number of them gorgeous young women. Dylan didn't quite know how the young women of America had suddenly decided stock car racing was sexy, but he wasn't complaining. To Dylan, they made his job a lot more interesting.

There was at least a vanload of college girls crowding him now as he made his way to the garage, but he didn't mind. They all had long hair and bare legs. Sure, the hair color was different, and some bared their legs with little bitty skirts, and some wore butt-hugging shorts, and unless he learned their names he'd have trouble telling them apart.

The blonde whose T-shirt read NASCAR CHICK told him her name was Tiffanny, with two *N*s. "Where y'all from, girls?" he asked as he obligingly autographed a ball cap with his number on it. Some women gave him a hard time for using terms like *girls*, but he wasn't going to stop. Political correctness was so complicated he'd pretty much given up trying to figure it out. He believed to the depth of his being that women should get paid the same money for the same work as men, that they could pretty much do anything they pleased. However, he also believed it was his God-given responsibility as a man to treat women with a little special courtesy, and if a young woman in a miniskirt wanted his autograph, then she might have to put up with him opening a door or pulling out her chair for her or calling her a girl.

"California," she said, all suntanned legs and long blond hair and not looking at all that offended he'd referred to her and her friends as girls.

"Long way from home."

"We came specially to see you," she said, as she'd no doubt say to any other driver she could stop. "Are you going to win on Sunday?"

"Honey," he said, "I am going to do my very best."

Then he posed for a photo with the bunch of them and took the next item shoved under his nose. As he signed a copy of today's newspaper, he wondered idly how many dorm rooms had his picture tacked up on the wall and shrugged.

Who could figure celebrity?

He made sure all the kids in the vicinity got an autograph, and then with a final wave and a "thanks, folks," he walked past the guards and back into the garage where his crew was already crawling over his car like ants over picnic leftovers.

"Hey, Dy," Mike Nugent said. "Me and the crew are going for dinner and a couple beers tonight. You coming?"

"Can't. I'm going to a wedding."

"Who do you know getting married in Charlotte?" Mike asked.

"Ashlee."

The older man blinked slowly. "You're going to your ex-wife's wedding?"

"It's kind of a tradition. I've been to all of 'em."

He and Mike had known each other for years. His crew chief regarded him with eyes that had worked on metal chassis so long they'd taken on the color of steel. "Make sure you don't end up as the groom—again."

Ashlee, his ex, had gone on TV twice now claiming he and she were getting back together. Both times it had come as a big surprise to Dylan. Probably a bigger surprise to the poor sap she was set to marry tonight.

"I've got it covered."

"Why do you let her get away with this stuff?"

He thought about it. "Ashlee's trying to find a way to be happy. I wasn't much of a husband, so if she wants to have some fun at my expense once in a while, who am I to blame her?"

"Dy, buddy, she wants you back."

"Not going to happen."

CHAPTER TWO

KENDALL KNEW her disastrous day had sunk another notch when she accidentally locked herself out of her hotel room.

In her underwear.

Unable to believe she could have been so easily bested by a fire door, she tried the knob, pushed her hip against the door, but it remained sullenly closed.

Kendall wasn't the sort of person to walk out of a door without ensuring it stayed open for her safe return. Stress and shock, she discovered, could do strange things to a person. Added to the natural stress of being dumped by her fiancé on the very day she was to receive the greatest compliment of her career was the rising panic that she'd miss her moment of glory. She hadn't come all the way to Charlotte to accept the Sharpened Pencil Award in her underwear.

Embarrassment prickled along her skin as she stood there for a moment wondering what on earth to do. She'd only stepped outside to see if her dress was back yet.

Breathe, she told herself, determined not to panic. She was top-to-toe ready, so the minute the dress arrived—and she found someone to let her back into her hotel room—she'd grab her clutch purse and her neatly typed acceptance speech and go.

A minute ticked by. Two. The air felt overwarm and she heard the faint noises of a large building, but saw no sign of her dress. There was no hotel phone on her floor. Could she slide into the stairwell and creep downstairs, then somehow get a hotel employee's attention?

Yes, she thought. That's what she'd do. Tonight would be the culmination of her career and she couldn't be late—especially since her ex and his recently outed love would be sure to think she was moping. Her chin went up at the thought. She might have a broken heart, but she was hanging on to her pride with every ounce of willpower.

At last, the sound she'd been waiting for—the whir of the elevator and then the *clunk, shhhh* as it stopped at her floor. She jogged forward, anxious for clothing. Ahead of her, a room door opened and a man came out, luckily without looking her way, at the exact moment the elevator doors opened. Horror of horrors, over the man's solid shoulder she saw three of the regional managers from her company—including her own boss—step out.

Kendall didn't stop to think. In one smooth gesture—and a surprisingly quick one, thanks to the panic-driven adrenaline suddenly coursing through her veins—she stuck her hand out and caught the door the stranger had exited from before it closed.

Then she slipped inside the unknown man's room.

Even as she sagged in relief, having whisked herself out of sight before the trio of managers saw her, she knew what she was doing was wrong. Thankfully, this room door didn't seem to be as efficiently quick at slamming behind a person as her own, but that was no excuse for trespassing. Still, she only wanted to use his phone to call down to the front desk and get someone to track down her dress and another room key. And this time she wasn't giving up until she was certain her request had been understood.

She walked down the short hallway past the bathroom and closet into the main part of the room, idly noting a black case on a luggage stand and a pair of dirty socks on the floor. She averted her eyes as though that would minimize her rude intrusion into another guest's space.

Perhaps she should write the stranger a polite note explaining her behavior....

Or would it, in fact, show better manners if she—

Her etiquette dilemma ended when she got to the main room and found a man there. It had never occurred to her that there could be someone else inside. Before she could open her mouth to apologize, he glanced at her and said, "You're late. I'd about given up on you."

Kendall blinked stupidly as she looked up at a man who seemed vaguely familiar. Not another actuary. Something about his air of danger told her he didn't calculate risk for a living. He was only a couple of inches taller than she was in her heels, but muscled and hard-bodied. There was a scar on his cheek that seemed unnecessarily large— as though it was showing off what a tough guy he was.

"I'm so, so sorry," she stammered. "I would never normally enter someone else's hotel room—"

"No problem. I'm glad Mike let you in. I was waiting for you. Come on, let's go." He looked her up and down in a way that suddenly reminded her she was still in her underwear. "Nice dress."

"It's a slip."

"Never can get the hang of ladies' fashion terms. Looks good on you. Sexy." He picked up a light gray suit jacket and pulled it on over matching slacks and a crisp white shirt, which clearly suggested somebody in this hotel got their clothes pressed in a timely manner. He wore no tie, but his black shoes shone.

Sexy? He thought she looked sexy? Some of her embarrassment at being caught in a slip faded. Okay, quite a bit.

He walked up to her and put an arm around her shoulders, turning her toward the door. At his touch she experienced the strangest sense of weakness. He had the kind of energy that could carry a person with it, whether she wanted to go or not.

When they got to the door, she realized she had to stop him or she'd be back where she started—out in that corridor with no clothes. She turned. "Um, just a second."

He reached around her for the door handle. The door at her back and Mr. Muscle in front was the absolute definition of being stuck between a rock and a hard place. His jacket just brushed her arm and as he looked down at her she noted his eyes were a deep, mossy green with brown-and-gold flecks. "What's your name?"

"Kendall Clarke," she said and foolishly stuck out her hand.

"Kendall. Do you go by Ken? Kenny? K.C.?" He spoke with the syrupy drawl that suggested he was from around these parts.

She shuddered. "I most certainly do not. It's Kendall."

Solemnly, he shook her hand. "Pleased to make your

acquaintance." He didn't say ma'am, but the accent implied it. "You seem a little uptight there, Kendall. Everything all right?" The way he said her name, it sounded like Ken Doll.

"If I could use your phone?"

"No time. You can phone from my car. Come on."

"Your car?" She put a hand to her head, partly to see if it was still attached to her body. Too much had happened today. The tug of familiarity when she looked at him didn't help. "Who are you?" she finally asked.

Amusement flickered in his eyes, fascinating her. "I thought Bryce was going to fill you in. My name's Dylan. My friends call me Dy."

And thunk, it all fell into place like three cherries in a slot machine, although of course she'd never play a slot machine. You didn't have to be an actuary to figure out that the odds were stacked against the player.

That's why he'd seemed familiar. Dylan Hargreave was a NASCAR driver. And not just any driver. He'd caused the kind of sensation even a non sports buff like Kendall had noticed. "You're ranked fifteenth so far this season." It wasn't that she followed sports, but rankings and number systems of every kind appealed to her and sort of stuck in her brain. There were a lot of numbers stuck in there.

"Wait till Sunday, honey. All that will change. This speedway's my track." She felt his intensity like an engine revving. "Bryce said you were a fan."

"Bryce said that?" Whoever Bryce was.

"Sure. I promise tonight won't be too boring. We'll have dinner, make nice, and be on our way. We can catch up to Bryce after if you like."

She felt as if she were in a dream; everything was a little misty around the edges and didn't make any sense. "This is a date?"

His smile crinkled the corners of his eyes and made that scar turn from a wobbly *L* to a *C*. "You're right. It's not a date, exactly, more an acting job. I sure do appreciate you being able to make it."

She'd always thought Southern men had more than their fair share of charm, but this guy was in a league all his own.

NASCAR driver, Actuary of the Year, acting job. It wasn't adding up.

"Can you handle it?" This man regarded her from those mossy-green eyes as though she weren't the brightest spark. How extraordinary. She supposed he had ample reason to doubt her intelligence, given that she'd stumbled into his room half-dressed and seemed to echo every statement he made. For a few luscious moments, she was experiencing what it might feel like to be a silly woman. Not silly, she reminded herself. Sexy.

The kind of woman a virile and exciting man like this might look at twice.

He stared right into her eyes a moment longer and she took that as a good excuse to stare back. Rough, tough and gorgeous. His hair was a tumble of dark brown with the kind of streaky gold that suggested he spent time in the sun. His skin was weathered, the mouth uncompromising, the jaw cleft. And that scar fascinated her.

"I don't want to be rude, but do you really need Bryce to find you dinner dates?" The guy was great-looking, successful, rich. He didn't look like the sort of man to need help getting female companionship.

He scratched a spot behind his ear. "Bryce was supposed to explain all this. I needed an actress. You just hang all over me, pretend we're crazy in love. For a couple of hours at this wedding we're going to, I want people thinking I have a girlfriend. That's all."

"I'm to appear as your girlfriend without actually being one?"

"That's right. Can you handle it?"

She laughed at the bitter irony of her situation. "Oh, yes. I've had practice."

He glanced at a watch that looked designed for a scuba diver rather than a race car driver. "We'd better get going."

Not much of an explanation, but she really didn't have time to get into this guy's relationships with women.

Now was the time to tell him that Bryce hadn't sent her, she was wearing a black silk slip from Victoria's Secret and that no one was ever going to mistake her for a NASCAR driver's girlfriend.

She was the kind of woman that the man she'd been dating for two years dumped on a business trip so he could sit at the actuary banquet with his pregnant girlfriend.

And suddenly the thought of slogging through dinner alone, while Marvin and Penelope canoodled in some dark corner, was simply too pathetic. Kendall had a secret romantic streak. She gobbled up novels and subscribed to a couple of movie channels including an oldies station. She loved the moment, especially in old films, when the enraged heroine slapped the out-of-line guy, when she stood up and said, "Nobody treats me this way."

Maybe all that reading and viewing hadn't been a waste of her time, as she'd sometimes thought. Maybe it was training for her moment to stand up and slap Marvin—metaphorically, of course.

A thought struck, so utterly blinding in its brilliance and daring, that her heart jumped unpleasantly.

The NASCAR driver standing in front of her at this very minute believed she could pass as his girlfriend. Why on earth couldn't she see what that would be like?

On the heels of that thought came another, even more scintillating.

What if she showed up at her banquet with this walking shrine to testosterone? This man, she suddenly recalled, who'd been featured in *People*'s 50 Hottest Bachelors issue. Wouldn't that show Marvin—and everyone? Not exciting enough, huh?

What if she talked Dylan Hargreave into dropping by her awards dinner? The voice of reason that had stopped her doing anything crazy, or even remotely interesting, for the thirty-one years of her life, said in a snide, evil-stepmother voice in her ear, "In your unmentionables?"

She ignored the little snide voice. Not giving herself time to think this through, since, if she did, she'd do the sensible thing, she said, "I have an event myself I need to attend here in the hotel later on. Could we be back here by, say, ten?"

She was scheduled to receive her award after the dinner and speeches. The agenda said ten-fifteen, and based on her knowledge of previous awards dinners, the award would be presented precisely at the time indicated.

"Sure. It gives us an excuse to leave. What's your shindig?"

"I'm receiving an award," Kendall said, not without pride.

"Cool. An acting award?"

She ought to get one for this performance. She did her best to look enigmatic. "I'll explain later."

What was she doing? she asked herself again as they walked down the hall toward the elevator. There was no answer forthcoming. All she knew was that she liked the feeling that she could pass for the date of the Sexiest NASCAR Driver Alive. She felt his energy and laugh-in-the-face-of-danger personality beside her. That personality was so big and so strong she felt it spilling over and imbuing her with craziness. She had no purse, no room key, nothing. Not so much as a tissue. She'd never done anything this wild in her life. Oh, it felt good.

The elevator doors opened on a couple kissing so passionately the mirrored walls had steamed up. The man had pale blond hair and wore a suit. The woman wore something black and low cut at the back. Even before the man lifted his head, Kendall was tugging Dylan's big hand and turning for the stairs. She recognized that suit. She'd been with Marvin when he bought it in the January sales last year.

"Let's give them some privacy," she said in a low voice as she tugged.

"Kendall?" Marvin sounded like a man who couldn't believe his eyes. Jerk.

"You know that guy?" Dylan asked as the fire door shut them into the stairwell.

"No," she said. It was true. She'd never known Marvin, not all the time she'd dated him, helped him get ahead in the company. He'd seemed as dull as she was, which made him a safe risk. Or so she'd thought. As it had turned out, he was a bad risk, one she'd have to write off. As though her life were an insurance policy.

Her heels clicked defiantly as she ran down the stairs, echoing like hail while Dylan's heavier tread sounded like a drum.

By the time they'd clicked and drummed their way past the reception floor, she had to admit she had completely lost her mind. She wasn't getting off to go and pick up her dress and her room key, and she wasn't going to the awards banquet to sit meekly with the other onesies.

She was blowing off the banquet.

Predictable and safe hadn't worked out so well.

She wondered what wild would feel like.

She had a feeling she was about to find out.

CHAPTER THREE

DYLAN WAS SURPRISED at the woman Bryce had set him up with. Bryce's female friends were a fairly predictable type. Gorgeous, friendly, long-legged and big-bosomed. This one was different.

Sure, she was sexy in a quirky-looking way. Generous mouth, straight nose, pretty gray eyes. Medium-brown hair that curled softly round her shoulders. Nice, trim body. Not much shape, but then he'd never known an actress who didn't diet off her curves.

Oh, well. All she had to do was act happy to be in his company for a couple of hours, then they'd be on their way. How hard was that?

Truth was, it was a lot tougher than he'd thought being named one of *People* magazine's 50 Hottest Bachelors. That had been great for publicity, and he sure sold a lot of junk with his picture on it. He also signed a lot of autographs to girls who looked as though they should be home studying for their algebra tests and not at a racetrack hyperventilating over guys who made a life's work out of driving too fast.

A lot of drivers took their wives and girlfriends around the racing circuit with them. Dylan had never done that. He'd come up in racing right when it

suddenly became a sexy sport. His marketing guy liked
him to have a different girl on his arm at every track. It
was a part of his "brand," whatever that meant. His
marketers wanted to portray Dylan as a fun guy who
loved women. Dy had no problem with that. He *was* a
fun guy who loved women.

He met some great gals: cheerleaders, actresses,
models, party girls. They got publicity from being seen
with him, and he got the sexy rep without any effort on
his part. Seemed to him that everybody went home happy.

For tonight, however, he needed something more.
Anyone who'd already been seen with him on TV or
mentioned on one of the fan sites wasn't going to cut
it. Ashlee would know the relationship was casual. And
he needed her to believe, for both their sakes, that he
was in love. He hoped Kendall was a hell of an actress,
because they were appearing before a tough audience.

KENDALL HAD her first major pang of regret when she
saw the car.

Low-slung, red and topless. The man was a race car
driver—he was bound to go over the speed limit, and
excessive speed accounted for a high percentage of
motor-vehicle accidents.

She paused. In the fluorescent lighting bouncing off
gray pavement, that red car looked like blood in the
desert. She scented danger.

She halted. There was still time to go back.

You're not exciting enough. Marvin's words floated
into her head as though he were standing beside her re-
peating his obviously rehearsed goodbye speech.

Not exciting enough, huh? She'd show him exciting.

Dylan unlocked her door and opened it and she slid into that car as though she rode in sports cars every day of her life instead of her four-year-old Volvo.

The engine roared to life in an aggressively loud fashion, and she wasn't pleased to note that Dylan pulled out of the parking space before she'd found her seat belt and clicked it into place.

The car purred as he steered out of the parking garage, but it was a menacing purr, as if to say, "Just you wait until I'm out on the road, baby, then you'll know fear."

They pulled out of the garage and she swallowed a cry as he merged into heavy traffic with hardly a glance. She'd never realized a topless car would be so noisy. And what it was doing to her careful hairdo she didn't even want to think about.

"So," he yelled over the wind rushing through the convertible, "I know you're an actress and you're here in town shooting a commercial, but where are you from?"

"Portland."

"How long are you in town for?"

"Three days. I leave tomorrow." And then she'd be back to her regularly scheduled life, in the job she'd done now for eight years, the apartment that she'd be deMarvinizing when she got home. When she thought about it, there wasn't even much of Marvin there. An extra toothbrush and razor, the shampoo for thinning hair, a couple of pairs of socks and underwear. An asthma puffer. So little. Some fiancé. Had there been signs all along that she was temporary and she'd simply ignored them?

They turned onto a freeway and her date hit the accelerator. The noise increased; wind rushed at her so fast she felt breathless. Her hair whipped across her face.

There wasn't much more conversation; it was too difficult to be heard. Besides, she was busy holding on to her hair so she didn't end up with lacerations on her face. She tried not to calculate their speed and turned her mind instead to cataloging ways she might fool people that she was: a) an actress; b) sexy and c) wearing actual clothes.

The sun was a low, heavy ball of dark orange. Dylan had slipped on dark sunglasses, but she, of course, had none. Between driving into the sun and the air whooshing at her, her eyes began to water.

They drove maybe half an hour and then they drew up at a big, old mansion decked with twinkle lights. Jay Gatsby would have felt right at home. Perhaps, as her first effort as an actress, she should channel Daisy.

Dylan roared toward the front of the house, and a white-coated valet immediately came forward to open the car door. She stepped gratefully onto solid ground, resisting the urge to drop to her knees and kiss the pavement. She put a hand to her hair to try and smooth it. The young man parking cars seemed more interested in her chest than in her hair, however, and when Dylan walked around to join her, leaving the car running, she noticed his gaze headed in the same direction. She glanced down.

The cold, rushing air hadn't merely unhinged her hair and made her eyes tear. She didn't know whether to put her hands to her hair or her chest, or simply to dive back in the car and refuse to come out.

Before she'd made up her mind, her attention—everyone's attention—was caught by a sylphlike young woman in a long, white off-the-shoulder dress, who cried "Dylan!" and ran down the stone steps as though a murderer were after her. She carried a bouquet of flowers in one hand, a lit cigarette in the other, and there was a coronet of tiny roses in her bright blond hair.

Kendall saw that her eyes were large, her lips pouty in a way that would have looked sullen on Kendall but looked sexy on this woman. She had a lost-child look about her, combined with a blatant sexuality. In fact, Kendall didn't have a hope of channeling Daisy. This woman had the channel all to herself as she threw her arms around Dylan and clung like a climbing rose to a garden stake.

"Hey, Ashlee," Dylan said in a voice that was soft and comforting, "it's good to see you." He ran a large hand up and down the woman's delicate spine. "You got some great weather for the big day," he said in an overly loud voice.

The bride shook her head so violently that her curls bounced and one pink rosette slid from its crown. "I can't go through with it. I'm making a terrible mistake. I never should have left you. Never. My astrologer said I'd end up with a man from my past. You've got to stop the wedding so we can get back together."

Kendall felt as though she'd been kicked somewhere in the region of her belly button. He'd brought her as a date to his ex's wedding? Was she forever going to be the one standing on the sidewalk of life while the parade passed her by? *She* wanted drama and astrologers and a man like Dylan letting her cling like superstrength sandwich wrap.

Instead, she felt exactly like what she was: a half-dressed actuary at the wrong party.

Mentally calculating how long it would take her to get back to the hotel in a taxi, she idly watched as Dylan patted Daisy with one hand and managed to pinch her cigarette out of her fingers with the other. "And it broke my heart into a million pieces when you did leave me. But Harrison's a fine man. He can give you all the things I never could. You know that."

"No." Another rosebud tumbled as the curls were tossed again. "No. I know it was you she meant. I know it. Let's get back together again." She glanced up with misty eyes.

Over the blond head, Dylan stared at Kendall and opened his eyes wide in a do-something plea. She'd been frozen in place by the spectacle—as had all the parking valets and a couple of guys in aprons who looked like catering staff on a smoke break.

Dylan wanted to be rescued from this lovely woman? By her? She felt better by the second.

Right, she reminded herself. Actress. Sexy. Pretend she and Dylan were in love. Well, if she wanted to take part in life's drama, it looked as if this was a perfect opportunity to step onstage.

She barely knew what she was doing when she licked her lips, thrust her hips forward and walked—no, strutted—forward into the fray.

Daisy didn't notice her. All her attention seemed to be given over to clinging to Dylan.

The parking attendant's attention was all hers,

though, or her still-chilled chest's. "You might want to park that car before it runs out of gas," she said in a throaty voice she barely recognized.

A reflex apology for her curtness popped into her mouth like a hiccup when she realized that the parking attendant had blushed to the roots of his red hair and was jogging to the driver's side of the sports car. Emboldened, she turned to do her best to free Dylan.

She'd succeeded in getting Daisy's attention. She had Dylan's attention, too. He still patted Daisy, but his gaze was fully on Kendall. She wasn't sure what to do next but she'd agreed to come with him and play her part and she was a woman who stood by her word.

"Who is this?" Daisy asked sharply, sounding a lot less fragile.

"This is Kendall, my—"

"Lover," Kendall said—or her inner vamp did, and she just mouthed the word. "And if you'd take your hands off Dylan, I'd appreciate it."

"This is your new girlfriend?" Daisy stared at Dylan as though she could not believe it.

"I'm crazy about her," he said, sending Kendall a glance so warm she tingled all over. For a second, she felt the thrill of those words run through her system. No man had ever said he was crazy about her, and even though she knew Dylan was pretending, she still felt as though she'd become someone new and sexy and powerful.

"But she's so…slutty."

Kendall blinked. In high school, she'd been voted least likely to go skinny-dipping. Now she was being called slutty? The sensible part of her knew she should be insulted, but her inner rebel, who'd never before appeared to exist, cheered.

"Ashlee, I am crazy in love with this woman. I want you to be happy for us. Like I'm happy for you and Harrison." There it was again. Not only crazy, but crazy in love. She wasn't the only one who seemed to have hidden acting talent. Mr. Dylan Life-In-The-Fast-Lane Hargreave wasn't bad in the acting department himself. When he looked at her with sizzle in his gaze, she felt as though he could not wait to get her alone. When he looked at her like that, she saw how easy it would be to respond.

With incredible dexterity he somehow unwound himself from the clinging bride and took Kendall's hand in his. His palm felt warm and large. Nice. He squeezed her hand in what she knew was gratitude. "Kendall's an important woman in my life so I want you to behave."

"Hi," Ashlee said, then glanced up under her lashes at Dylan and gave that sexy pout again. "Sorry I said you were slutty."

"Hi," Kendall replied. "Sorry I thought you were a bitch."

Dylan made a choking sound and quickly faked a cough. Then he spoke to Ashlee. "Now let's get you married."

Kendall could not imagine who was going to marry this woman who was so blatantly throwing herself at another man, but she'd already realized that the rules of Dylan's world were vastly different from her own. Then she thought about Marvin and realized that wasn't true at all.

Ashlee looked as though she was going to argue or, worse, cling some more, when thankfully another car drove down the avenue toward them. The bride-to-be squeaked and ran for a side entrance to the mansion.

She stopped halfway, turned to Kendall and yelled, "I'm Dylan's first wife. You know the first marriage is the only true one."

Dylan held on to Kendall's hand as they walked up the stone steps to an imposing oak doorway. "Thanks for that. You're a better actress than I guessed."

"Better than I would have guessed, too," she admitted. None of this was her business, but she had to ask, "Will there be many more scenes like that?"

"I hope not," he said, and she was sure she felt him shudder.

"Are you sure it's a good idea for you to attend your ex-wife's wedding?"

"It would hurt her feelings if I didn't show. Besides, me coming to her weddings is kind of a tradition."

"Weddings?"

"This is number four."

Dylan kept hold of her hand as they ascended the main staircase leading to the house. To an onlooker it would have appeared they were inseparable, but Kendall suspected he was afraid she'd bolt if he didn't hang on tight.

He needn't have worried. She was enjoying more excitement tonight than she'd experienced in her entire life. She wasn't going to miss this crazy wedding for anything. Her gorgeous, sexy date didn't, however, have to know that.

"You didn't mention that our date was to your ex-wife's wedding," she said sweetly.

"Huh. Must have slipped my mind."

They walked into a blaze of light and noise, a string quartet almost drowned out by the chatter and laughter of a great number of well-dressed people. The mansion reminded Kendall of the Biltmore Estate she'd visited near Asheville. This mansion had the same feeling of Gilded Age glamour, and although not quite so over-the-top, was still pretty amazing with its art deco architecture and old-world interior decorating style. She'd only gotten into the Biltmore as a paying tourist. To be in a Gilded Age mansion as a guest—however bogus—was quite a thrill. She was again reminded of Gatsby as she glanced around, drinking in the atmosphere. Of course, Fitzgerald had lived in the area. Perhaps he'd visited this very house.

A woman spotted them immediately and came forward. She was an older, faded version of Ashlee, wearing a soft pink suit and a corsage of orchids. "Why, Dylan," she cried, holding out arms that didn't just drip diamonds; it was more like a waterfall. "We'd almost given up on you, and you know Ashlee planned her wedding around the NASCAR schedule so you could be here."

Good move, Ashlee.

Kendall didn't think she was ready to face the mother of the bride. She hadn't yet recovered from meeting the bride. She mumbled something about the washroom in the general direction of Dylan's ear, and stepped away as his ex-mother-in-law enveloped him in a hug that looked mildly incestuous.

The washroom was a grand affair, of course, with black-and-white tile, marble walls, crystal chandeliers and acres of mirror. The sight of her reflection made her cry out in distress. Her first ride in a convertible and she'd learned a valuable lesson. Never travel without a hair net. Her hair was big, windblown and hopelessly tangled. Any of her makeup that hadn't been whipped off by her hair flying around her face at far too many miles an hour had smudged, run and spread so she looked like a rocker chick who'd gone a few rounds with a tornado.

Never mind she was prancing around at a society wedding in her underwear, her carefully styled hair and makeup were a mess and she had not so much as a clutch purse with her. No comb. No makeup. Nothing.

Fortunately, the washroom was equipped with wonderful Deco jars of stuff, so she sat on the blue velvet bench in front of a marble vanity and reached for a silver-backed brush, refusing to even think about how unsanitary it was to use a hairbrush of unknown provenance, age or cleanliness. This was an emergency.

Redoing her softly curled style was out of the question, but once she'd brushed it out, her hair had a certain wavy wildness that could be considered deliberate. Pinching off a single tiny orchid from the gorgeously blooming plant in a black-and-white pot, she tucked the creamy bloom behind her ear.

With a dampened tissue she managed to reduce her convertible-induced raccoon eyes to a kind of smudged shadow she hoped appeared intentional. Then, with a deep breath and a sense of fatality, she left the washroom.

Her few moments alone had given her the opportunity to realize that she'd gone temporarily insane. There was no other possibility. Marvin's announcement—that

triple whammy of 1) I'm dumping you; 2) for a colleague and 3) she's pregnant—had pretty much tossed
Kendall into unexplored mental territory.

However, she wasn't quite ready to head back to her
usual rational state. For one night, she was going to
enjoy a small vacation from her usual self. Appearing
for one night only was Kendall Clarke, actress and girlfriend of one of NASCAR's sexiest drivers.

She was determined to enjoy every minute.

Dylan was, by this time, in deep conversation with
an older man. He must have kept an eye out for her, for
when she reached his side he didn't even turn, merely
put an arm around her and pulled her close.

Mmm. His chest was broad and warm. She sensed
the power and strength of his athlete's build. Really, not
much acting was required for her to lean into his
embrace and gaze up at him as though he was the most
exciting man she'd ever met.

"Clyde," he said, sending her a shadow of a wink that
only she could see. "I'd like to introduce my girlfriend,
Kendall. Clyde is Ashlee's father."

"It's a pleasure to meet any friend of Dylan's,"
Clyde said. He was a dapper man who looked to be in
his sixties. He was balding, with salt-and-pepper hair
and a neatly trimmed moustache. Ashlee may have
thought Kendall looked slutty, but her father saw
nothing amiss. His eyes twinkled when he looked at
her. "A pleasure indeed." She felt Dylan's arm tighten
around her.

She smiled at Ashlee's father and shook his hand,
which he held on to a little longer than necessary.

Ashlee's mother came over and said to her husband,

"Now, don't monopolize Dylan. Our other guests want to say hello." Then she stood there and engaged her daughter's ex in conversation herself, leaving Kendall stuck with the husband, who moved a step closer.

"What a lovely dress," he said, doing his best to look down the front of it.

"Thank you."

"I do like these skimpy fashions you young women choose."

"A recent study of media photos revealed that female stars bare approximately fifty-nine percent of their bodies today in public appearances as compared to a mere seven percent in the 1970s." She sighed. "No wonder the fitness craze keeps getting crazier."

The older man blinked. "What is it that you do, my dear?"

Oops. Shut up with the statistics, she reminded herself. "I'm an actress." More seemed to be required, so she added, "Shooting a body lotion commercial."

"You know, I've always been interested in how they make commercials. I'd love to come by and watch you work."

"Oh, I don't think that would be allowed," she said as brightly as she could.

He chuckled softly. "I've got a lot of connections. Which company's shooting? I tell you what I'll do. I'll come watch you work and then I'll take you for lunch at my club. I'm sure you'd enjoy it. The chef's famous. He has a way with steak that no one can duplicate."

As an actuary, she dealt with a lot of older men and she had her own method of dealing with the overfriendly.

"That's very kind of you," she said with a smile,

"but I shouldn't encourage you to eat red meat. You know that a man of your age who eats large amounts of red meat has a sixty-four percent greater chance of developing heart disease than a similarly aged vegetarian. Of course, you're increasing your risk of type two diabetes by fifty percent." He gaped at her and she went in for the kill. "And don't even get me started on the stats for prostate cancer and colon blockages."

He paled and the smirk left his face.

She patted his arm. "I wouldn't want to put you at risk."

"Right. Um, yes, of course. Well." He stared at his drink, then put it down on a nearby table. "I'd better see how…everything's progressing. Mabel?" he said sharply to his wife. "Come along."

She glanced up to find Dylan looking at her in a quizzical way. "That was one of the most colorful brush-offs I've ever been privileged to witness," he drawled. "How'd you know all that stuff?"

Darn, she'd hoped he hadn't heard.

She shrugged. "*Scientific American* was all they had in the green room."

He glanced at her curiously. A waiter passed by with a tray of champagne and she took one, sipping deeply. Dutch courage, her mother would call it. She'd take courage of any nationality right now.

"Your beer, Mr. Hargreave," the waiter said. Dylan studied the bottle of beer, nodded and waved away the empty glass provided.

"Thanks."

"You don't like champagne?" How could anyone not like champagne?

"It's okay, but my contract states that the only alcohol I can drink is my sponsor's beer."

"Isn't that a little restrictive?"

He shrugged. "They don't put their money behind any other drivers and I don't drink anybody else's booze. Works for me."

Dylan might have said more, but he was soon surrounded by people. He didn't seem too surprised; she guessed he was the most famous person in the room and probably used to being approached. People checked her out the way she imagined they eyeballed his race cars, wondering if she was up to his speed, pretty enough, sleek enough.

She was a Dinky Toy compared to his usual cars.

What was she even doing here? It was unlike her not to act sensible.

Then Dylan looked at her with a slight grin, and the scar crinkled so much she wanted to reach out and run her fingertip over the puckered curve. He was the kind of man a woman like her could only worship from afar. Now, for tonight, she belonged by his side.

Forget sensible.

CHAPTER FOUR

KENDALL DISCOVERED that when you acted as though you were interesting and fun and sexy, a lot of people went along with the charade.

Of course, being with Dylan pretty much guaranteed that people were going to form a different impression of her than they would if they saw her in her office in one of her Talbots suits.

And, strangely enough, the same phenomenon worked backward. The more that people treated her as though she were interesting, fun and born to party, the more of a fun party girl she became.

Wedding guests came up and talked to her, they told her jokes that made her laugh and she said things to make them laugh in return. Okay, they were all men talking to her, but that was all right. Her flirting skills were rusty—if she'd ever had any. It was nice to give them a workout.

Whether her newfound popularity with the opposite sex was because she was here with a NASCAR driver, barely dressed or had suddenly sprouted a sparkling personality, she didn't know or care. She was Cinderella at the ball with Prince Charming. Naturally, midnight would come and she'd soon be back to her regular unexciting life, with no glass slipper left behind to change her destiny. So what? For once she was following a mad impulse and to heck with the consequences. Not exciting enough, huh? How she wished Marvin could see her now.

Dylan came and took her arm, and since he was by far the most interesting man at the wedding, she beamed at him. "Isn't this a wonderful party?" she said. It was amazing. She could say the stupidest things and people thought she was a witty conversationalist.

"It's a nightmare," he said, not appearing to find her conversation all that witty. Immediately, the truth slapped her, and she in turn slapped a hand over her big mouth.

"Oh, I'm sorry. I forgot. This must be torture watching your ex-wife get married." And Daisy/Ashlee was exactly the sort of woman for whom a man would carry an eternal flame.

He glared at her in annoyance. "She won't get married if she doesn't believe you and I are crazy in love. So would you stop drooling on everything in pants and start drooling on me?"

Her mind was feeling a little hazy. It was thirsty work, all this flirting, and she was wondering if she might be one flute short of an orchestra. Or maybe that should be one flute too many. She'd stick with water at dinner, she decided. In the meantime she tried to work out what Dylan meant. "I don't understand what's going on. Are you still in love with her?"

"No!" He pulled her aside and in a low voice said, "This guy's her fourth groom. She went to some astrologer who I would personally love to strangle. This quack told her that she's already met the love of her life but she threw him away. She got it into her head that that man was me."

She'd seen Dylan and Ashlee together. Both were gorgeous, larger than life. They were Clark Gable and Carole Lombard. "Maybe the astrologer was right."

He shook his head. "Our marriage was a disaster."

"Still, you've never married again."

"I'm smarter now." He glanced behind Kendall and his eyes narrowed. "Uh-oh, here she comes. If I know that look, and I do, she's planning something crazy. Like not getting married so she can run off with me. Remember, this is your fault."

As she opened her mouth to ask what exactly was her fault, he kissed her.

Oh, my....

Better than champagne was the first thought that skittered through her head. His arms came around her and pulled her in so tight she was pressed against the full length of him. Oh. Yum. Oh yes, oh yes, oh yes.

He was sexy and strong, and in that second she could imagine a woman loving this man and never wanting to let him go. Then Ashlee/Daisy fled her mind as he kept on kissing her. He tasted good, felt good. Her arms went around his neck and she molded her body to his. With nothing between them but her slip, a demi bra and a pair of panties, she felt the roughness of his jacket, the buttons on his shirt, the warmth of his skin.

A soft moan startled Kendall back to reality. For a humiliating moment she thought she'd done the moaning, but when Dylan raised his head and looked behind her, she turned and followed his gaze. It wasn't Kendall who'd moaned, but Ashlee.

The bride was staring at Dylan with a baffled mixture of longing and sadness. "I remember when you used to kiss me like that," she said.

"That was a while ago," he said, but in a gentle way. He kept his arm around Kendall and rubbed her arm, up and down, while he said it.

"I just want to be happy," Ashlee said, her big blue eyes looking misty. Kendall wondered if she'd ever heard anything so wretched. If the woman was wondering about her happiness on her wedding day, then it didn't bode well that she'd found it.

Since this didn't seem to be one of those weddings where it was deemed bad luck for the groom to see the bride before the ceremony, Kendall soon had a chance to judge the upcoming union for herself.

A self-important young man strolled up and Kendall was reminded again of Gatsby. This guy was a modern-day version. She couldn't have said why she thought he was from new money until she looked more closely. His tux was too obviously expensive. His shoes too shiny. When he took Ashlee's hand, he held it in such a way that an extraordinarily large diamond engagement ring winked at them, catching the light and flashing like a camera bulb going off.

Ashlee smiled at her fiancé, but then turned her attention back to Dylan. Kendall could understand why. He was much the more dynamic of the two.

"Hargreave," the nouveau Gatsby said with a curt nod.

"Bryant." He nodded back.

Animosity crackled between these two. No one bothered to introduce her.

"The minister's here," the groom said. "Your mother wants you to take your place."

"Okay." Ashlee's voice wobbled and she looked at Dylan with such naked appeal that Kendall hoped someone would protest the marriage. Preferably the groom.

"Be happy, Ashlee," Dylan said and, stepping in front of the man she was about to marry, kissed his ex-wife on the lips.

The groom took Ashlee's hand and dragged her away, and she left with the same enthusiasm a child leaves Santa's knee.

"Well, you kissing her silly should cure Ashlee of her infatuation," Kendall said.

"Bryant irritates me," he said, as though she might not have noticed.

"Why?"

"Harrison Bryant went to a big, fancy university and learned all about higher profits through downsizing. He'd done some hatchet jobs on other companies and was seen as a young hotshot who'd take the old factory in our hometown and make the shareholders happy. A real wunderkind. Our town was already suffering a downturn. The factory is still the main employer in town, but he's cutting jobs so fast nobody can keep up. It's wrong, that's all."

"Did you know each other before…?"

"Before Ashlee? Oh, sure. We all grew up together. That's what made it so bad that he'd come back and destroy his own home."

It was an old love triangle, then. She wondered how far back it went. "I've heard of him, of course. No one could believe the way he turned around that steel company in Pennsylvania or—"

He stared at her.

Right. Not the sort of thing most actresses would need to know. She was going to have to tell him who she really was. But not quite yet. Not while that kiss was still fizzing through her system and he was displaying her to these people the way Harrison Bryant had displayed Ashlee's diamond ring. So she shrugged.

"They stock *Barron's* along with *Scientific American* in the green room?" he asked.

"The wedding's about to start," she said, nodding to where a stream of guests headed into the conservatory.

Kendall hated confrontation of every kind and so her stomach was one big knot when they took their places in the conservatory. The scents of gardenia and frangipani were everywhere.

Still, the conservatory was beautiful with tiny white lights in the trees and a single harpist playing by candlelight. They sat in rows of white folding chairs, on the bride's side. After an interval of shuffling, some quiet whispering and the odd giggle, the parents filed in to the front row. Then Harrison Bryant seemed to appear from behind a burning bush, although she imagined there was a side door behind the blooming gardenia bush that was currently imitating a candelabra. With the groom was an older man, presumably the best man. The thought flashed through her mind that he didn't have any friends his own age.

The two took their places in front of a flower-decked podium while a man in a dark suit holding an engraved binder came from the other side and took his place behind the podium. When the justice of the peace had found his place in the binder and adjusted the small reading light, there was the usual anticipatory prebride silence.

Kendall waited, barely breathing, for the groom to be left standing at the altar—a fear the groom apparently shared from the anxious way he kept glancing behind him. But, soon enough, the "Wedding March" played and in came a flower girl with a mass of blond curls and huge blue eyes, enjoying her importance so immensely that there was a snowstorm of flower petals wherever she went.

Behind her came two bridesmaids who looked as though they had better things to do, and finally Ashlee, who gnawed her lip all the way down the aisle.

However, no one, not even the bride, tried to stop the wedding. When the justice of the peace announced, "You may kiss the bride," she felt Dylan's arm droop slightly as his muscles relaxed and she realized he'd been as tense as she.

AFTER THE WEDDING came a sit-down dinner reception. Usually, when Kendall went to a big do, she and Marvin were close to invisible. Conversation tended to stall when people found out they were both actuaries. But Dylan's table felt like the table at the center of the universe.

He was hailed, backslapped, joked with, teased and flirted with so often she wondered how he managed to get any food down. He bore it in good part, managing to charm the women, talk racing jargon with the men and still find time to fiddle with Kendall's hair, place an arm around her shoulders, whisper supposed secrets in her ear.

His behavior kept her on edge and fluttery, so it was

hard to eat anything. Since one of his whispered intimacies was to remind her that she was supposed to be crazy in love, too, she let herself do what she'd wanted to do all evening. She traced the shape of that scar with a fingertip. She felt the tiniest thread of scar tissue and a slight dent. His skin was warm and beneath the pads of her fingers she felt the slight scratch of stubble. When she would have removed her hand, he took her wrist and kissed it.

Her pulse jumped as though it wanted to kiss him back.

Down girl, she reminded herself. It's pretend.

As she made her way through the high-class version of banquet rubber chicken, she felt a stab of guilt. She should be at her own actuarial dinner eating the plebian version of rubber chicken. Marvin's behavior didn't abnegate her responsibility to her employer. If only her *ex*-fiancé had told her earlier, given her time to get used to heartbreak and humiliation, she might have handled this evening with her head instead of her damaged heart.

Maybe her behavior wasn't entirely appropriate, but so long as she got to the banquet before the speeches, she doubted she'd be missed.

While the ritual wedding toasts were made, she kept an eye on her watch.

The first dance between the bride and groom had Kendall blinking in surprise. Ashlee seemed to have forgotten all about Dylan and for this dance, anyway, she had eyes for no one but her latest husband. And Harrison looked as though he cradled the most precious being in the world. Why, that man was the one crazy in love, Kendall thought. She hoped he didn't end up heartbroken.

It wasn't a great feeling.

A glance at her watch told her it was nine. After the actuary dinner, which would be winding up about now, coffee would be poured and there would be the usual speech from the president of the association that had never been clocked in at shorter than sixty minutes.

"I should really get back to the hotel. I need to get my acceptance speech from my room."

"Fine by me. Let's get out of here."

Since they'd been snuggling all evening, she wasn't at all surprised when he took her hand. A woman could get used to this guy, she thought. And this woman better not.

They made their way unimpeded out the front door, which made her sigh with relief. Probably it was rude to leave without saying goodbye, but in Dylan's case, goodbye undoubtedly took hours.

"So, you'll definitely come to my banquet with me?" she asked as they walked out into the still, warm air of a May evening.

He glanced at her, and a tiny frown pulled his brows together. "What exactly is this award?"

"Does it matter?" If she told him the truth about herself, she felt as though all the magic would drain out of the evening.

Dylan glanced up at the night sky twinkling like a sea of glitter. "See, the thing is, I'm a broad-minded guy. But I've got sponsors. Fans." He glanced at her and looked a little embarrassed. "I hate to be acting like a prude here, but if you're adult movie actress of the year, or something—and believe me, when I say that I think it's a great honor—then I'm going to have to pass."

"Adult movie…?" For a second she was stumped, then she sucked in a breath. "You mean pornography?"

"Hey, listen, I'm all for good, clean fun in the privacy of your living room but, like I said, I've got to be careful…."

She turned to him. "You think people would pay to see me in sex movies?"

"Absolutely."

"Thank you," she said, feeling better than she'd felt all night. "But I am not a porn star."

That crooked grin was aimed her way and with it the crinkling of that scar that for some reason made her weak at the knees. "You kiss like one."

She tamped down her delight with feigned severity. "And how would you know how a porn star kisses?"

His evil chuckle was drowned out by the approaching sports car. The low, red car zoomed up and Dylan opened the door for her, then walked around to tip the valet and slide into the driver's seat.

She found herself back in that convertible flying along the highway a million miles an hour.

When she tilted her head back to look up at the sky, it was like a kaleidoscope where the pattern kept changing too fast for her to keep up.

"So, are you going to tell me what this award's about?" Dylan yelled over the combined noise of the road and the wind.

"No. Not yet. But I promise it's perfectly respectable."

"I'm trusting you here, Kendall."

"Trust," she said emphatically, "is the cornerstone of good business."

"You know, honey, you are an interesting woman.

You talk like an accountant with the same mouth that kisses like a porn star."

"Well, trust me, all resemblance to a porn star ends with kissing."

He laughed and threw an arm around her shoulder. "Why don't you let me decide?" That's when she realized he had misconstrued her meaning.

She blinked at him. He appeared more than pleased by the notion of having sex with her. In two years Marvin had never looked that interested.

But then, Dylan had only known her a few hours, and he thought she was someone else.

Was it her imagination or did they travel back to the hotel a lot faster than they'd traveled to the wedding?

Impossible to tell, but before she could believe it, he was pulling up in front of the hotel. Oh, cool. He was using valet parking. She felt rich and important as she slid from the car, while yet another parking attendant held her door open for her.

"Good evening, Mr. Hargreave," the doorman said, then nodded to her. "Miss."

When she swooshed through the door and found herself in the main-floor lobby, she blinked. There was the illuminated sign confirming that the actuary banquet was in ballrooms A and B.

"Where are you going?" Dylan asked as he fell into step with her.

"The actuarial banquet. I'm going to take a peek and make sure I have time to run upstairs and grab my speech."

He studied the sign, then glanced at her. "You're kidding me."

"No," she said, feeling like Cinderella would have if

she'd transformed back into the dowdy drudge before Prince Charming's eyes.

Instead of looking disappointed, or jumping into his race car and zooming off, he tipped back his head and laughed, a big, booming sound. "This, I have to see."

Most of the doors to ballrooms A and B were shut, but she found one that was propped open. She crept toward it and stuck her head inside. Amazingly, the president had kept it short this year. He was winding things up. There was no time to get herself another key and run upstairs and get her speech. She'd barely made it here in time.

Oh, well. She'd practiced her speech so many times, she'd mostly memorized the thing, anyway.

The president of the actuary association of America was praising someone who exemplified all the qualities of the best actuary.

"This year's winner combines a keen mind with exceptional organizational abilities. She's been top…"

"What are we doing here?" Dylan whispered, coming behind her and kissing her neck.

"Basking," she said. "And keep doing that."

"Ladies and gentlemen, it's my pleasure to present this year's Sharpened Pencil Award to Kendall Clarke."

"Hah," she said, tipping her head back to smile at Dylan. "Talk about good timing."

"This is your award?"

"Yep. I'm Actuary of the Year. I have to give a speech. Kiss me for luck?"

He did, and the tingle on her lips was just the fuel she needed to make the long walk to the podium.

All the dark-clad men and women at all the tables in ballrooms A and B were clapping.

They were clapping for her. The tiny voice that had ruled her, sleeping and waking, for so many years, was throwing some kind of hissy fit, but she couldn't hear it over the sound of polite applause.

CHAPTER FIVE

SHE WALKED to the microphone and there was the president of her organization, Gordon Carstairs, staring at her as though he couldn't believe his eyes.

Mr. Carstairs had been a friend of her father's and ran the only insurance company in Portland larger than the one where she worked.

"Thank you very much." She reached forward to kiss him, Hollywood-style, and he pushed the award forward, Actuary Association-style. The sharp point of the trophy, a sharpened pencil, poked her right above her heart. Somehow, that seemed significant.

She stared out at all those dark suits and dresses, all those white-moon faces staring at her.

"Ladies and gentlemen, guests, colleagues." Pause. Breathe. "Trust is the cornerstone of our business."

Trust. The word seemed to shimmer in her mind so each letter sizzled neon.

"Trust." She repeated the word, hearing it echo around the still, waiting room.

Three hundred ghostly faces stared at her. Marvin sat about three tables from the front. Through some trick of the overhead lighting, or maybe the fluorescent bounce of his pale blond hair, he stood out.

If she scanned her gaze to the left, to the entrance and exit to the ballroom, there was Dylan, standing with his back against the wall, watching her.

In that moment, everything inside her went still.

The silence lengthened to become a palpable thing—something you could feel in the air, like humidity. She heard some shuffling, and a couple of cleared throats. Somewhere, somebody started chatting in a low voice.

She felt dizzy, and realized inside her she'd sailed blindly into the perfect emotional storm.

She glanced at the Sharpened Pencil Award she'd placed on the podium. So straight that pencil was, so sharp. And she started to speak.

"I am honored that you would choose me for this prestigious award, but I can't accept it."

Actuaries weren't the most emotive of souls, and there was not so much as a gasp from the audience. She noticed that the chatting stopped, though, and the silence felt keener.

She smiled. "I know these speeches are usually pretty boring. Let's face it, our jobs are pretty boring, but what we do is important. Without us and our calculations, retirees could run out of money before running out of life. Insurance companies would go bankrupt if we didn't calculate risk. What we do matters."

She took a sip from the glass of water that had been provided.

"I talked about trust, but there's more than just trust involved in being a good actuary. We also need to act with integrity and good judgment."

She looked straight at Marvin. "I've always prided

myself on my judgment, but somewhere I went badly wrong. I became engaged to a man who has been carrying on with another woman under my nose. We three are colleagues in the same office, and I was clueless."

She shook her head, appalled. She had everyone's attention now.

"I think a person who is so blind to the kind of deceit and drama going on in her own life might not be sharp enough to catch discrepancies in her work."

She paused to sip more water. Her hands were surprisingly steady.

"Trust, integrity and good judgment are three cornerstones." *And what kind of judgment are you showing now?* an inner voice railed.

"But a building has to have four corners or it will topple. Honesty is, I think, the final piece. I have lived dishonestly for the last four months, through no fault of my own except blindness. My colleague and fiancé informed me earlier this evening that he's in love with someone else. I've been blind, foolish. I've been living a lie. So, you see, I am the wrong person to accept this award, although I hope one day to be worthy of it. Thank you."

And she turned and walked slowly away, leaving the sharpened pencil pointing in the air like a rude middle finger.

DY WATCHED his date of the evening with a combination of shock and admiration.

Okay, so he'd already pretty much figured out that Bryce hadn't sent her and she wasn't like any actress he'd ever met. But her speech still shook him to the toes.

She'd been dumped by a cheating fiancé if he understood her speech correctly, and was refusing an award that probably meant a lot to her—on ethical grounds.

Wow.

He'd pretty much written off the evening as a nightmare before it even started. How had he ended up having such an amazing time?

There was something about this woman, with her quiet sexiness, her clear intelligence and her obvious integrity, that got to him.

He wondered why the evening had been so different than he'd imagined and then it hit him. He hadn't been bored.

Boredom had been a part of his life so often recently that it was like an allergy—he'd become so used to it that when the symptoms cleared up he felt incredible relief.

Of course, not a soul in the world knew about this problem of his. Only a loser would whine when he had everything he'd ever wanted.

And he wouldn't do that. He'd flipped the bird to his family, his predestined future and pretty much the world a lot of years ago and set out to prove himself.

Here he was, with everything he'd ever wanted. And if sometimes it all got to be too much of the same old, same old, then he'd suck it up and shut up. Faking being on top of the world was pretty easy when everybody already accepted that that's where you were sitting.

But when had he last laughed from that ticklish place deep in his gut that had been so accessible as a kid and so unreachable now? He couldn't remember. Until tonight when his supposed party girl had announced she wasn't an actress at all, but an actuary.

No wonder Kendall had kept him the opposite of bored. Between grabbing him back from Ashlee, slapping down his ex-wife's dirty old daddy and now standing up there and pretty much blowing off her career because of her principles, she not only amused him, she won his admiration.

When she came off that stage, the applause was tepid, the glances sent her way were everything from confused to disbelieving.

She appeared more shocked by her behavior than anybody. She looked like a rookie after a first major race. She was pale and shaky and looked as if she might puke.

What she needed was for somebody to take her mind off the ordeal. "Hey," he said. "Great speech."

"Thanks."

"Would it hurt your career any if I kissed you?"

"I think I just threw away my career," she said in a voice of stunned shock.

"Then I guess this can't hurt." And he leaned in and kissed her. What was it about this mouth of hers that he found so irresistible? It talked smart and kissed sexy. He was barely aware of the hundreds of people in the room except that he wanted them all gone and to have Kendall alone. He raised his head and she said, "Let's get out of here."

He grinned at her. "You must have read my mind."

"Kendall," a man said in a furious tone. He and Kendall both looked back at the guy he recognized from the elevator. The nervous-looking redhead clinging to his arm must be the one he'd been kissing. "How could you be so small-minded and…and vindictive? You made a fool out of me."

Dylan's date looked at the guy for a long moment and said, "No. I didn't. You did that all by yourself."

Dylan scooped her hand into his and they left without a backward glance.

"What do you want to do now?" he asked her as they crossed the mostly deserted lobby.

"I'm thinking of locking myself in a bathroom somewhere, then throwing up and doing a lot of moaning."

He chuckled. "No, you're not. You totally impressed me. Probably a lot of other people, too."

"I did?" Her eyes were serious but with an edge of dreaminess he liked.

"Yeah. You told off a whole roomful of suits and you never raised your voice once. If I was the president of that association I'd be getting your ex's ass fired and making you CEO of the company."

The line between her brows disappeared. "You would?"

"Yep. You're the one with guts and integrity."

"Thanks." They walked a little farther. "You're right. We have to celebrate. I did something I've never done before. I stood up for myself and told somebody off."

"You've never done that before?"

"Not really. Well—" she glanced at him "—Ashlee, earlier tonight, but that was acting."

"I have to say, you're doing great for a beginner."

"Thanks." She sighed and gazed up at him. "You know what I want to do now?"

"What?"

"I want to do something else I've never done before. Do you have any idea how many things I've never even tried?"

He was curious as to what she'd say. "No."

She started listing things off on the fingers of one hand. "I've never scuba dived, even though I love the ocean."

"Well, we're kind of far from it here. And they don't let you go out if you've had a drink or two."

She gasped. "And that's another thing. You know I've never been drunk?"

"Didn't you ever turn twenty-one?"

"Of course I did. But I was studying for final exams. I couldn't waste a whole study night to go drinking."

"Now that is just plain tragic."

"Where are we going?" They'd walked outside the hotel. The air was warm and dry. Even though it was dark, he slipped his sponsor's shades on, hoping the suit and the sunglasses would make him less recognizable. There were so many race fans in town for Sunday that he was liable to be mobbed if he was recognized.

"I figured out the perfect thing for you."

"Something I've never tried before?"

"That's right. I'm guessing you've never raced a stock car before."

"No-o-o." She licked her lips and gazed up at him, that little line appearing between her brows. "I thought I'd move my way up through my list. Starting with easy things. I'm not sure I should be racing quite yet."

"Trust me. You'll love it."

"OH MY GOSH, I clipped him. Aaaaggh! I'm going too fast. I can't hold on. I'm going to crash."

Dylan was getting as much of a kick watching Kendall play the new NASCAR video game as she was playing. Her fingers were welded to the controller and her eyes wide as she stared at the moving images on the screen.

She'd never be a beauty, but there was something very appealing about the way she gave her whole focus to what she was doing, whether it was playing a video game, telling off her ex or kissing him.

When she'd played four games in a row, she finally threw up her arms and gave up.

There were six of them at the table—his crew chief, a few guys from the team and Carl Edwards, a little younger than Dy, but he'd become a good friend. They'd both been featured in *People*'s 50 Hottest Bachelors issue, and what had started out as good-natured ribbing about which of them was really the hottest had turned into a friendship.

Since Carl was a lot better at video NASCAR, he'd taught Kendall. By the time she'd mastered the basics, they were fast friends, and he was toasting her success. "Kendall, you're a natural." He glanced at Dy with that grin that melted a lot of female hearts and signaled to Dy that trouble was on its way. "We should get her a ride, Dy. She'd be a great driver."

"Are you kidding? I crashed three times, lost control once and I'm pretty sure I made the yellow car blow up."

"Sounds like a good day on the track to me," Carl said with that toothy grin a lot of women seemed to go for.

Kendall laughed as though Carl was the funniest guy in NASCAR. He had to be a few years younger than she was. Carl didn't seem to mind, though. In fact, Dylan might have to remind his fellow driver to find his own woman before the night got much older.

CHAPTER SIX

KENDALL WOKE to the sound of moaning. Unfortunately, she was the one doing the moaning.

She'd drunk champagne at the wedding and then had a beer while playing that video game. She was definitely what people referred to as a cheap drunk. Maybe she ought to winnow that list of "never dones" before embarking on too many more firsts.

Underneath her pounding head and slightly rocky stomach was a feeling of persistent euphoria, however. Last night she'd been the kind of woman she admired. Strong, adventurous—Dylan Hargreave had called her kick-ass.

She quite liked that view of herself. Of course, in the racing world, being kick-ass was no doubt a good thing. In the actuarial world, she wasn't so sure.

No one in history had ever refused the Sharpened Pencil Award. It had felt like the right thing to do when she'd stared right at Marvin and his pregnant girlfriend and realized how incredibly blind she'd been, but had she gone too far?

She rolled out of bed, showered and dressed. Today she was going home. Back to her life, her job and the humiliating reality of facing her ex-fiancé's new love growing rounder every day with his child.

To think that twenty-four hours ago everything had been so different. She'd still been blindly engaged, arrogant enough to think she deserved the Sharpened Pencil and had never met a NASCAR driver in her life.

Dylan. What an extraordinary date he'd turned out to be. Sexy, funny, gorgeous. Aloof. She suspected he was an easy man on the surface and one it was very difficult to really get to know. He'd helped make sure she got her key when they returned to the hotel in the wee hours, and he'd given her a brief but scrumptious kiss outside her door.

She hoped he hadn't left Charlotte yet. She wanted to say goodbye.

She could phone him but—no. She should thank him in person for the fun she'd had last night. As she reached her hotel room door, someone knocked on it.

Her pulse jumped. Dylan? Was he thinking of her as she was thinking of him?

When she opened the door, her regional manager, Bob Bream, was standing there. With him was the VP of human resources, Glen Sugorsky.

"Oh," she said in surprise. "Hello. Would you like to come in?"

"If it's convenient."

"Of course."

It felt very strange to have two of the muckety-mucks from her company in her hotel room. She wished more than ever she'd passed on that beer last night. She had a feeling a clear head was going to be called for.

"Sorry to barge in on you like this, Kendall," Bob said. He was a fussy little man with a bald head and thick glasses who kept his desk so clean dust didn't dare settle.

Glen was tall, with an athletic build going to fat. He had thick lips and a ready laugh.

"That's all right." She glanced around. There were two chairs at a small table under the window, and a third chair at the small desk where her computer sat. "Please sit down."

She carried the chair from the desk closer to the table.

"Thank you. We would have liked a more conventional meeting space but—" Glen raised his hands "—we gave up all our meeting rooms. And we wanted privacy."

"Really, it's fine." She was all packed since they were leaving today, so the room was as impersonal as any meeting space if they all turned their backs to the bed.

"Well." Bob was obviously the designated speaker at this meeting and he seemed as though he wasn't sure where to begin.

Her churning stomach now had nothing to do with the alcohol.

"Kendall, your speech last night was a, um, surprise to all of us. I…we…those of us in senior management had a meeting this morning, in person and conference call. We agreed that your speech—your behavior, in fact—was inappropriate."

Her feeling of being a kick-ass woman began to dissipate faster than snow beneath a blowtorch. "Perhaps you're right. I admit I didn't intend to say what I did. I should have taken more time to think it over."

"Yes," Glen agreed. "You should've."

"As I'm sure you realize," she said, "Marvin Fulford and I—"

"Yes, indeed. A very distressing situation. Marvin

came to us last night, very upset. He held nothing back. We want you to know, Kendall, he was candid that his relationship with Ms. Varsan made you very emotional."

Anger swept through her like a brush fire. "He broke our engagement less than an hour before the banquet. I wasn't emotional. I was betrayed, angry, heartbroken."

"The situation, as I'm sure you can understand, is untenable. We simply cannot have these kind of personal dramas affecting our work."

"Of course not," she agreed. "I assure you that I will do my job, as I always have, with the utmost professional integrity. However, I have been blind not to see what was going on under my nose. It was that lack of perspicacity in myself which made me refuse that award. It wouldn't have been right to accept it."

"Nevertheless, your speech publicly embarrassed our company and one of our senior employees."

"An employee who has been humiliating me for months behind my back." She had to stay calm, she reminded herself even as her voice shook.

"Kendall." Bob went for the avuncular tone. She supposed he thought he had the right to treat her like a child. "I've known you a long time and I believe you've got a wonderful future ahead of you."

"Oh, good." She breathed out. "I thought for a second there you were going to fire me."

Bob cleared his throat and looked at the blank table as though searching for something to straighten or tidy. "Of course not. However, we are a respected firm. We cannot allow people involved personally to affect the workplace."

"Then you might want to separate Marvin and Penelope."

"We're moving Ms. Varsan to Payroll. She's accepted the new position."

"Where are you moving me? The mail room?"

Glen spoke up. This was obviously his leg of the dog and pony show. "We're transferring you to the branch office in Aurora. You'll be assistant branch manager."

She blinked. "That's a storefront insurance office that isn't even open yet. I'm not an insurance clerk. I'm an actuary."

"I'm sorry, Kendall, but we think this is for the best. As you point out, the Aurora location won't be viable for a few months. We're offering you a three-month stress leave. When you return to work, you'll report to the Aurora office."

"Stress leave?" She stared from one to the other. "You think I need a stress leave?"

The silence was so thick she heard Glen's shoes scrape the carpet as he shifted.

"And Marvin?"

"He'll remain where he is. We feel we've solved the problem."

"But Marvin was the problem."

"This isn't open to discussion, Kendall. The decision has been made."

She looked from one to the other, unable to believe what she was hearing. Marvin kept his job, and the two women he'd been involved with got demoted? She was sent off on stress leave for three months? "What if I refuse?"

"Your position has been relocated to Aurora. You have no job in the Portland office."

All those years. All that training. The hours she'd put

in, the loyalty she'd felt for the company. It was so blatantly unfair, sexist and wrong that she felt like screaming. An outburst that would only confirm their obvious
conclusion that she was too emotional.

"So you're demoting me."

"Not at all. This is an excellent opportunity to learn
another part of the business. Consider it a sideways
promotion."

She wanted to tell them to take their measly
sideways promotion and shove it sideways. But she
had thirty-one years of good-girl behavior against one
short night as a rebel.

There was no contest.

Dylan was looking for a missing sock when his cell
phone rang.

"Dylan?" the soft voice of his ex-wife greeted him.

"Ashlee? Aren't you supposed to be on honeymoon?"

"Honestly, Dylan, you never listen to a word I say."
He'd heard that line often enough when they were married.
"Our plane to Nassau doesn't leave until Thursday."

"Right." There was a pause. Since he was the ex-
husband, asking about her wedding night didn't seem
appropriate, although he couldn't think of anything
more inappropriate than her calling him on her first
morning married to another guy.

"What's up?"

"I wanted to tell you how happy I am that you've
found someone special. At first I thought she was awful,
but then I saw you two kissing and I could tell that you
and Kendall are totally in love." Her voice lowered.

"It's the only thing that made me go through that ceremony last night. If you're happy in love, then maybe I can find it, too."

Oh, great. He and Ashlee had had a pretty wretched marriage, all told. Between the yelling and the scenes, her being in love with the excitement of what he did and then freaking out before every race, there'd been little peace. Then there was the issue of her being a spoiled little rich girl and him being an equally spoiled little rich boy. They hadn't stood a chance.

Still, he harbored a stubborn affection for Ashlee. She was flighty and spoiled, but she was also sweet. When she'd said she wanted a divorce, he'd felt nothing but relief. It took him months to realize that when she'd thrown those words at him she'd been loving the drama and expected him to talk her out of leaving. In the three marriages between, she still hadn't given up on getting back together. He was fairly certain that she was drawn to the excitement of his world, but what she really craved was stability. He also wished she'd figure out soon that she didn't love him any more than he loved her.

However, to blow her off would be like kicking a little Persian kitten for scratching up the upholstery. He couldn't do it.

Ashlee's biggest problem was that she was a born fool for romance. Being a three-time loser at marriage hadn't dampened her sentimental notions an iota. Usually her starry-eyed romantic routine irritated him, but in the case of him and Kendall, he was glad Ashlee had decided to see true love where none existed. Kendall might not be a real actress, but she'd ended up doing a good job last night of acting crazy for him.

"I am telling you, Ashlee, that woman means the world to me. Like you mean the world to Harrison."

"I know. I'm so happy for you. She seemed really slutty at first, but maybe that's the kind of woman you need," his ex-wife said with no irony that he could detect.

"Yeah, well, it might be a good idea to stop calling her a slut. I don't think she appreciated it."

"I guess it was prewedding jitters. Look, honey, if she's going to be a part of your life, she's going to be a part of mine. Put her on the phone, will you? I want to apologize."

"Um, she's in the bathroom right now."

"Oh. You're not just saying that, are you? Because if she's right there and doesn't want to speak to me, well, I'll have to drive over there and apologize in person."

"No. No! Don't do that."

"But she'll be at the race tomorrow. I'm bound to see her. I want everything smoothed out now. You know how I am. I worry."

"You're going to the race?" What was wrong with Harrison that he couldn't grab his wife and get the pair of them on their honeymoon like a normal couple?

"Sure. You're in town, I'm in town. Why wouldn't I go?"

"Because you're on your honeymoon," he reminded her.

"That's silly. Harrison loves racing. We're all from the same town. We should support each other."

Oh, like that was going to happen.

"Let me talk to her, Dylan."

"The shower's still running. I should warn you that she's a bit of a clean freak. Once she gets in that shower, I swear she shampoos her toenails. She'll be a good few minutes yet."

"Okay. I'll talk to you until she comes out." She sighed. "Wasn't that a beautiful wedding?"

In Dylan's top ten things he hated discussing, "beautiful wedding" would make the top three. "Sure was. Where's Harrison? Shouldn't you two be makin' babies or something?"

"I sent him off to the jewelry store to get my wedding ring made smaller."

"Why didn't you go with him?"

"Because I wanted to talk to you and Kendall without him listening in, that's why. He thinks I'm having a facial."

"You're a spoiled brat, you know that?"

"Of course I know it, and so does Harrison. He'd do anything for me."

"He's a fool."

There was a short pause. "You're not going to make me mad enough to hang up on you so quit trying. Is Kendall out of the shower yet?"

He grabbed his room card and stuck it in his pocket before slipping out of his hotel room and into the hall.

"She's singing the 'Hallelujah Chorus,' so that means she's shaving her legs. She's almost done."

"Good. So, did you think the ceremony was too short? I didn't want to make too big a deal of it, being it was my fourth wedding and all."

Two hundred guests and enough candles to light up outer space wasn't a big deal? "No," he said. "I thought it was perfect."

From long experience, he knew he could make mmm-hmm noises periodically and Ashlee would keep talking. Right now she was going on about twinkle lights. Twinkle lights! "Mmm-hmm."

He banged on Kendall's door, hoping she'd still be there.

"Who is it?" he heard a minute later, in a tone that sounded as though she were expecting a firing squad.

"Honey," he said, loud enough for her to hear him through the hotel door, "Ashlee is on the phone. She wants to talk to you."

A beat passed.

"Honey?"

The door opened.

He blinked. "Kendall?" He'd barely have recognized the woman standing in front of him. She was dressed in a dirt-colored suit with a turtleneck the color of mould underneath. Her shoes were the flat kind favored by old women with bad knees. Her hair was neat and her posture stiff. What had happened to last night's wild woman?

Even her eyes had changed. Last night, they'd been sparkly and daring; this morning, they looked far too old for a young woman.

"What is it?" he asked, forgetting for the moment why he was there. He felt an impulse to wrap her in his arms. If anyone had ever needed a hug, it was Kendall.

She shook her head. "Is there something I can do for you?"

Right. The phone. "Ashlee wants to speak to you."

"She does?"

He nodded. He didn't have the heart to tell this model

of propriety that Ashlee was about to apologize for calling her slutty. He simply handed over the phone.

She hesitated and he mouthed, "Please?"

"Hello?"

After that there was a pretty long silence from Kendall's end. A simple "I'm sorry" from Ashlee was going to take at least fifteen minutes. Since he didn't feel like waiting out in the hallway, he nudged past Kendall and went to sit on the armchair in the corner of her room.

She followed him in, the phone still held to her ear. There was an open suitcase on the bed with a lot of suit-type clothes neatly folded. He'd never seen so many colors inspired by mud.

"That's all right. Really. I quite understand. No offense taken."

Then her gaze flew to his and she blushed. Ashlee must have got to the part about them being crazy in love.

Kendall crossed to the bed and sat primly on the edge, beside the open suitcase. "Oh, well…" She faltered.

He jumped up. She'd better not undo all that good work from last night. "Come on, honey," he said loud enough that Ashlee could hear. "Get off the phone and come back to bed."

"Oh, I know," she said weakly, shooting him a glare that she hadn't put much effort into. "Yes. Insatiable. You, too. Goodbye."

Kendall hung up, then handed back his phone. She looked a little stunned, but at least she had some color back in her face.

"So, you did a good job last night. She thinks we're totally in love."

"That's nice."

"Nice? It's fantastic. You saved me. Thanks."

She hung her head. "I impersonated someone else, went out on a date in my underwear, gave a speech the actuarial association will never forget. Don't thank me."

He chuckled. "That speech was fantastic. I was proud to know you."

He shoved the suitcase out of the way and sat beside her on the bed, putting his arm around her shoulders. "Forget that bunch of dull suits last night. Your acceptance speech was probably the most fun any of them have ever had."

She shuddered against him. "Some of those dull suits were my bosses. First thing this morning I was given a 'sideways promotion,' which is weasel-speak for I've been demoted."

"What?"

She nodded, still looking down.

"Well, that's plain stupid. I hope you told them to take their lousy job and shove it."

She sighed and fiddled with one of the latches on her case. "We live in very different worlds, you and I. Mine is all about risk assessment. Up until yesterday, I was an asset to my company. Today I'm a liability. I'm risky. If I could embarrass my bosses at an organization function, then maybe I'd do the same at a board meeting. My company is very conservative. They've taken steps to minimize damage. They say I'm being moved for my own good and they probably mean it."

"They're messing with one of their best people—or do they give that pencil to anybody?"

"No. You're right. It's a very prestigious award." She

looked at him and there was a crease between her brows. "So why didn't I simply tell you who I was when we first met last night, get my dress, go to the actuarial banquet and give the speech as scheduled?"

The question seemed a no-brainer to him. "Because you wanted to have some fun, and there was no way fun was going to be had at that corporate dinner. I about went into a coma from entering the room. It wasn't until you got going that the place livened up."

She put a hand to her head. She had dainty hands, he noticed, with long fingers. Her nails were longer than he would have expected, too, and painted pink. "Maybe they're right and I showed poor judgment."

"Maybe your ex should keep it zipped."

She glanced up and laughed, giving him a glimpse of the woman he'd had so much fun with last night. Then she sobered. "The two women involved were reassigned. Marvin gets to keep his job. The old double standard is alive and well in corporate America."

He didn't even know how to respond to that, but he felt vaguely guilty simply for being a man. "What are you going to do?"

"Take the job. At least I'll have the security of a paycheck while I think about my options."

"You don't sound real thrilled at the idea."

"I'm not."

"Do you need the job that badly?"

A tiny smile tilted her lips but not a hint of teeth showed. "I'm an actuary. I calculate risk for a living. The first thing I did after I paid off my student loans was build an emergency fund equal to six months' salary. But it's easier to find a job when you already have one."

"You started a job by figuring out what the odds were on losing it?"

She nodded.

He scratched his jaw. She was still pale, but a little color was coming back into her cheeks.

"Why don't you tell them to shove it and take a few weeks' vacation, which, if you don't mind me saying, you look like you could use, and then you find another job?"

"In your world it may be that simple. Not in mine."

"Babe, when you screw up in my business, you end up turning cartwheels strapped inside a tin can going a hundred and eighty miles an hour."

She shuddered.

"So do something else. You're too much fun for that roomful of corpses last night."

She shook her head, then put a hand to her forehead as though she'd forgotten she had a headache. "You're wrong. I'm exactly like those corpses. You've unfortunately got the wrong impression of me from my behavior last night. Perfectly understandable. We make decisions about a person based on first impressions. I showed up in your room half-dressed, I—"

"I thought you looked great."

Those long fingers with the pink nails touched her turtleneck as though checking it still covered her up to her chin. Unfortunately, it did. "Thank you. The point is, our meeting was all in error and then I compounded that error by pretending to be someone I wasn't, for which I owe you an apology."

This woman was way too hard on herself.

"Bryce left a message. The woman who was supposed to be my date last night had an appendicitis attack. Honey, you saved my butt."

"Well. That's good."

"Why don't you take some time off? Stick around here for a few days. Watch the race tomorrow. You'll be doing me the biggest favor of my life if you hang on my arm and tell Ashlee more about how much you love me and how incredible I am."

She managed a small eye-roll, which made him grin.

"She's married now. What difference can it make?"

"Hah. Ashlee treats marriage as a temporary inconvenience. All she has to do is get it back into her head that the astrologer meant she was supposed to be with me and she'll do something like embarrass me on national TV. Really."

Kendall shook her head. "I'd like to help you, but I can't. I have to get back to Portland."

"Hey, I tell you what. Tell them you need a couple of weeks off. It will give them time to organize your move. Stick around until Thursday when Ash leaves on her honeymoon, then I'll fly you home."

She blinked at him as though he'd suggested she detour to the moon. "You'll fly me home?"

"Well, not me personally, but my plane will."

"What kind of plane?"

"A small Lear."

"I'm being offered a ride in a Learjet. I don't believe it."

He grinned at her. "It would be another first for that list of yours. And if you wear one of those slips tomorrow, you'll get on TV for sure."

That earned him a genuine laugh. "As tempted as I am, I can't."

Before he could argue, there was a knock on the door.

"Now what?" she muttered to herself in exasperation.

CHAPTER SEVEN

KENDALL'S WORDS were still echoing in her ears when she opened the door and got a big dose of exactly what she didn't want right now. Aggravation.

Standing outside her door, looking self-righteous and condemning, was Marvin.

Before she'd worked out how to handle this—her instinct was to slam the door in his face—Marvin was inside her hotel room.

He'd begun talking as soon as she'd glimpsed his face. "I hope you're pleased with yourself," he said, his usually placid tones jerky and annoyed. "What in—" He stopped short as he caught sight of Dylan, who seemed like a dynamic comic book hero with his tall, dark good looks and his imposing body.

Next to him, Marvin seemed like exactly what he was. A nondescript, desk-bound middle manager with nice blond hair and not another interesting thing in his appearance.

Her head started to pound. She glanced at her watch. She still had fifteen minutes until it was safe to take another dose of painkiller.

"I don't think we've met," said Dylan, holding out his hand as though Marvin might be a fan in search of an autograph. "I'm Dylan Hargreave."

Marvin, as caught in the restraints of polite behavior as she, shook the offered hand as briefly as possible but spoke to Kendall. "Why is he in your hotel room?"

She opened her mouth to explain and Dylan said, "Well, there's a stupid question if I ever heard one." His drawl was so good ol' boy it almost took him half an hour to spit out those words. The look he sent her as he said them almost made her bones melt.

Marvin stared from one to the other. "Did you sleep with him?"

The words seemed to echo around the room. Dylan didn't say a word but glanced her way with a tiny, self-satisfied grin.

"That is none of your business," she snapped. Then she stalked into the bathroom leaving the door open. She took one of the hotel glasses, ran water from the tap, shook out two pain pills and swallowed them fourteen and one half minutes before the instructions printed on the back of the bottle said it was safe to do so.

At the moment, a little analgesic poisoning seemed a small price to pay for relief from the pounding in her skull.

"I would never have believed it," Marvin said in outrage. He was doing such a great job of the innocent act that she was certain he'd end up getting promoted after he'd managed to dump her personally and screw her professionally in the space of a day.

"Well," she said, coming back into the room, "I would never have believed you'd start a relationship with one of our colleagues right under my nose. What do you want, anyway?"

"I feel it is my responsibility to the firm to ensure you get home safely." And in full view of everyone who was anyone in the industry. How had she never noticed what a toad he was?

"Well, aren't you the Boy Scout?" Dylan said, sounding like his mouth was full of grits.

He piled a couple of pillows up against the faux-wood headboard and plonked himself down on her bed as though he were planning to stay for a while.

"Marvin, I'm fine. Thank you. I'll see you downstairs."

"I wouldn't feel right leaving until he does," Marvin said, gesturing with a jerk of his head to Dylan.

"The thing is, I'm trying to proposition Kendall and it's tough with an audience."

"Oh, stop it," she snapped, beyond exasperation. "You're not—"

"I am," he said, suddenly rising to his feet and stepping close. "Take a holiday. You sure look like you could use one. You can see a couple of races. We'll have a few laughs, go home when you feel like it."

"But I've got responsibilities, ob—"

She became aware that hers was not the only voice speaking. Marvin talked over her. "You've got obligations at home. You've got to stop acting irrational."

When she talked about her responsibilities, she felt mature and needed. Why, when Marvin mentioned the same thing, did she sound like an old maid?

"I'll be fine," she said firmly. Then walked over to the door and held it open until her ex-fiancé left, muttering under his breath.

She turned to say goodbye to Dylan, and it was harder than she'd imagined to walk away from the only man in her entire life who'd ever mistaken her for an exciting woman.

"Dylan, I…" What? If you're ever in Portland? For a wild second she contemplated giving him her business card, but Portland was nowhere near the NASCAR tracks—which was only one indication of how far outside Dylan's world she lived. "I enjoyed meeting you," she said.

"I had a great time last night," he said, his voice low and sexy.

Their night out might have resulted in disaster, but she couldn't help the momentary spurt of pleasure when she recalled their evening. "I had a great time, too," she admitted, hoping she didn't sound too wistful.

"Bye, Kendall," he said, and pulled her to him and kissed her. He did something that made her shoulders and head tilt back and suddenly she was being kissed like she'd never been kissed before. A tiny sound came from her throat, kind of an oh-I-never-knew-it-could-be-like-this moan, and her arms went around his neck.

Suddenly, she wanted the clock to flip back to last night. She wanted to be in that foolish slip of silk, masquerading as the kind of woman a man like Dylan would parade on his arm. She felt her body tingle as the kiss continued. She'd have gone on kissing him for days if Dylan hadn't finally pulled away.

He looked a little dazed. She couldn't imagine how dazed she must appear.

"Here's my card," he said, digging one out of his pocket. "If you change your mind."

"Thank you," she said, accepting the small rectangle. Of course she wouldn't call him, but she imagined she'd hang on to this card forever.

He left and, after she'd carefully placed that card inside her wallet, she fixed her lipstick and wheeled her suitcase out of her room and toward the elevator, forcing herself not to look at Dylan's door when she passed.

She passed a housekeeper a couple of doors down from Dylan's room with a cart of cleaning products and bags of little soaps and shampoos. The woman nodded at Kendall and then pushed her dark hair behind her ears. There was a newspaper sticking out of a full trash bag and a headline about a presidential speech. Two things immediately struck Kendall as odd. One: she hadn't read this morning's paper—what with all the drama, there hadn't been time. And two: she didn't seem to care.

In that paper there was probably a whole lot of ink about tomorrow's race. She wondered if Dylan was mentioned and if her date would soon fade into one of those amazing celebrity encounter stories that don't seem quite real.

Thankfully, she was alone in the elevator. She made her way swiftly through the lobby, having used the express checkout and left her keys in her room. When she got outside, she noted that the air was warm, the skies sunny. There was a lineup of people standing in front of the hotel, each with a black bag or two. As her eyes focused, she realized that she knew most of them.

They were all members of the actuary association, people she'd hoped to avoid this morning. Now she remembered the chartered bus that had been booked to take the departing actuaries to the airport before they went their separate ways.

She greeted a few people as she walked to the end of the line, the wheels of her case bumping across the pavement.

Conversation wafted her way from some of the people standing in the line, bits and pieces of desultory chitchat which stopped suddenly. She turned slowly and saw Marvin and Penelope. They weren't holding hands, but they looked as though they'd only recently stopped.

They took a few steps forward, saw Kendall at the end of the line and hesitated in perfect synchronization. She glanced at Marvin and, as though realizing he couldn't stand there much longer without looking like an idiot, he started forward once more.

The two of them took their place in line behind Kendall.

Humiliation burned in her stomach. Some of these people were colleagues she'd known for years. They'd been on her wedding invitation list. How could Marvin do this to her?

"Um, Kendall?" Marvin said softly behind her. He sounded tentative and kinder than he had earlier. The thought flicked through her mind that he was going to apologize.

She had no idea how she'd respond, but an apology would be nice. Some admission that his behavior had been reprehensible would go a long way to soothing her lacerated feelings.

"Yes?" she said, turning to face him. She knew that every eye was on them and felt that she could one day forgive Marvin if he tried to smooth things for her today, on this most difficult of days.

A low roar that sounded familiar came from behind

her, where the cars exited from the parking garage. Marvin had to raise his voice to be heard above it. "I was wondering if you would mind changing seats with Penelope so she and I can sit together on the plane?"

Unbelievable.

Dylan's car appeared, a shiny red blur in her peripheral vision.

The line of dark-suited men and women stretched like a black rope that bound her to her past. Dylan's sports car was the future, a rocket ship to adventure. It was her getaway car.

They wanted to gossip about her? She'd give them something to talk about.

"Hey, Dylan," she shouted, stepping forward with her hand outstretched as though she were hailing a cab.

He slowed and pulled close to where she stood.

"Is the offer still open?"

He grinned at her, the dare in his eyes. "Hop in."

"Kendall, I strongly advise you to think about your behavior," Marvin was saying behind her, while all those curious, gossip-hungry eyes looked on.

In seconds, Dylan had stowed her luggage in the tiniest trunk she'd ever seen, then jumped back behind the wheel of the rumbling car.

They were pulling away when she heard Marvin shout, "Are you crazy?"

"Oh, yes," she cried, turning to send him a goodbye wave. "That's why I'm on stress leave."

Crazy had never felt so good.

CHAPTER EIGHT

"How do you feel?" Dylan glanced her way with the smile that made her stomach wobble.

"Shocked." She craned her head over her shoulder and saw the bus for the airport arrive. The bus that she ought to be on. For a second she contemplated begging Dylan to drive her to the airport, then she stopped herself. No. Maybe jumping into Dylan's car was a little wacky, but she'd made her decision. She could slink home with her tail between her legs and spend her "stress leave" miserable, or she could do something wild, crazy and completely exciting. Right or wrong, she was giving wild and crazy a try.

"I hope I have something appropriate to wear to a car race," she said. "I've never been to one before."

"Honey, if you want one man's opinion, your underwear is a lot nicer than those clothes I saw in the suitcase. They're all the color of dirt."

"Earth tones," she corrected. "I once had my colors done. I'm a fall. We're supposed to wear the colors of autumn—greens and browns and rusts," she explained.

His glance suggested that he hadn't been reminded of colorful autumn foliage when he'd looked inside her suitcase. The trouble was, she was never sure when a color was a verifiable fall-foliage tone and when it was a summer orange or a winter red. That's how she'd ended up with so many safe browns and beiges. How did she think she could handle a race car driver? She was a woman who couldn't even imagine a Color Me Beautiful clothing palate.

A mile or so passed and she saw that they were on a highway. She had no idea where they were bound. "I think I should explain that I'm not normally an impulsive person."

He glanced over and at the speed they were going, she really wished he wouldn't. He should keep both eyes on the road. And both hands on the steering wheel. "I think you have hidden depths. Last night you were definitely impulsive."

"Yes. I suppose I was." A flicker of pride glowed inside her. "I'm not sure why I did that. It's so out of character." That made it twice in two days she'd done something completely unlike herself.

"Why did you let that little pissant treat you that way?"

"Marvin?" She thought about Dylan's question. "I'm not very good at standing up for myself." She sighed. "In fact, I'm terrible." She nibbled her lip and looked out the window thinking about how often she'd berated herself for the problem and yet been unable to act any differently the next time she was asked to do something that wasn't her job, or had someone break in while she was talking, or refuse to listen to her ideas.

"Maybe all you need is some practice."

"I signed up for assertiveness training last winter, but it didn't help."

Dylan glanced over at her with a disturbing twinkle lurking in his eyes. "What happened? Did you fail?"

She bit her lip some more, wishing she hadn't been drawn into the subject in the first place. "I didn't go."

The twinkle in his eyes deepened. He wasn't stupid. "You were unavoidably called out of town?"

"No."

"Sick with the flu?"

"No."

"Trapped in an elevator?"

"Very funny. The truth is I was too scared to go."

"You know what I find interesting?"

She shook her head.

"You were assertive as all get-out at the wedding. Look how you handled Ashlee and her daddy. Maybe it's only with your own crowd that you act like a wimp."

She blinked. "I guess you're right." Then she shrugged. "I was playing a part, and since I'd given you my word that I'd act like...someone you'd be crazy about, I felt I had to present myself as much different than my normal self."

He chuckled. "Bit of a self-esteem problem there, have you?"

Oh, why couldn't she just shut up?

DYLAN PULLED AROUND a Camry with a Sunday driver at the wheel and his companion flinched. He stared at her. He wasn't one to brag, but he raced cars for a living. He had a couple of championship trophies on his mantle. If his streak of bad luck would only change, he might have a shot at the NASCAR NEXTEL Cup this year. Did she really think he couldn't handle a dry highway in the middle of a sunny May day with barely any traffic?

A few more miles went by and he managed to make her flinch several more times. It was starting to take the tedium out of the journey to watch her brake foot get a workout.

"Where are we going?" she asked him after they'd cleared Charlotte city limits and were heading south.

"The Speedway."

"Oh."

He glanced at her. "You ever watched a race?"

"Live, you mean?" She turned her face to his. "No."

"How about on TV?"

"Well, actually, no."

"You're going to be through that first-time list of yours by next week the way we're going." He thought of Kendall's upcoming reaction to her first race and wished he could sit beside her to see it.

"There's a lot of traffic."

"Welcome to race week."

"It takes a whole week? I thought the races only ran on Sundays."

"They do, but we go pretty much from Thursday to Sunday, forty weeks a year, what with testing and qualifying heading into the big race."

Her eyes were round as she took in the crowds they passed.

"Oh." She was silent for a while and he wondered how it all struck her. The motor homes and the beaten-up pickups, the families and the loners, the hard-core fans and the locals out for their one or two races a year.

"Hey, there's you!" she suddenly cried. Sure enough,

there was a flag with his picture and number on it. When they got closer and started passing the packed parking lots, she gasped. "Is that a margarita maker on the back of that truck?"

"Probably. Tailgate parties are legendary." The motor coach parks were packed, as usual, during race week. Some of the rigs were more expensive than the average house; others were old campers that had seen better days. Some fans brought along barbecues and planter pots and made a family vacation of it; others brought nothing but beer.

He got a real kick out of introducing a novice like Kendall to the sport he loved. He drove through to the infield where he knew his motor home would be parked. Now that he was here, he would stay on-site until the race was over. If he needed to get around, he'd take a golf cart. The high security gates were up and a guard was on duty.

"This is a secure area. Mostly drivers and their families stay here. We do get some race fans who pay a bunch of money for a spot in the infield. We need to get you a pass so you can come and go."

"Wow," she said, looking around her with interest.

His adrenaline started pumping as it always did when he entered the Speedway. He loved this place. He loved everything about it. The steeply tiered bleachers, the track itself, the buzz in the air.

He got close to the garages before he was recognized. "Hey, Dy! Hold up," a middle-aged male voice yelled, loud enough to wake the dead.

The cry soon became a repeated echo like a pneumatic drill. He tucked Kendall's hand in the crook of his left arm, told her not to let go and took out the pen he always carried in his breast pocket. Pictures, hats, scraps of paper, magazines, napkins—whatever was shoved his way he signed, keeping a smile on his face and talking to the fans as he went.

"Is that your girlfriend?" a boy about ten or eleven yelled.

His eyes met Kendall's and he shrugged. What can you do?

"She sure is, so you make room so she can breathe." Another one of his hats came over his shoulder, he signed it. "Five yards," he told Kendall in a low voice. Then they were at the garage and the guards were politely but firmly stopping the fans.

"Good luck, man," somebody shouted.

"Thanks," he said, giving a final wave and a grin caught by approximately two dozen cameras from the disposable kind to the semiprofessional film kind to the ubiquitous digital camera that would be beaming his and Kendall's pictures, along with the news that she was his girlfriend, to blogs and fan sites within minutes.

But that was part of the game and he tried to be a good sport, since those fans made the whole NASCAR thing possible.

"You okay?" he asked Kendall. She appeared shell-shocked.

"I know one in four Americans is a NASCAR fan, but you don't realize how many people that really is until they're stepping on your toes and shoving T-shirts at you to sign. Whew!"

He laughed. "Racing merchandise is big business."

He took her to his garage and introduced her to his

team, some of whom she'd met last night. If they were surprised to see her looking a lot more formal today, nobody said anything about it.

Jack Horsham, his marketing guy, was standing with Mike Nugent and glanced Dylan's way as he approached with Kendall at his side. "Finding your own women now, Dy?"

"The funny guy here is Jack Horsham," he said to Kendall, pulling her forward within the circle of his arm.

"Pleasure to meet you, Kendall."

"Hello," she said, and shook hands.

"She's going to be hanging out with me for a bit. I need you to find her a place to stay for a couple nights." He felt the tension in Kendall's body ease suddenly. What? Did she think…? Of course, she was still in shock that she'd blown off her paid ride home and jumped in his car without a Venn diagram of his plans, their itinerary and definitely some idea of the sleeping arrangements. Poor Kendall. For such a regimented, odds-calculating woman, this impulsive spree must about be killing her. He should feel bad, but he thought a little impulsive action would be good for her. He was, in fact, doing her a favor, just like she was doing him a favor by continuing to create a great big buffer between him and Ashlee. Hopefully, by the time Kendall went back to Portland, Ash would have made her marriage work, or found a new astrologer.

"We put a new engine in, Dy. She should be good."

He nodded and, telling Kendall to look around, soon had his head under the hood.

BY THE TIME they were getting ready to head out to the track, Kendall had met everyone and toured the hauler, being shown every lug nut in the pull-out fitted cabinets and every bag of junk food in the tiny kitchen. There was something about her air of serious interest that had the crew telling her a lot more than most visitors. He figured she'd learned about everything but the actual car, so he called her over for a look.

"There's no door," was the first thing she said when she approached the car, garishly painted with every one of his sponsors' logos. The main color was midnight blue, with a lot of red and orange. He thought he must look like a parakeet being shot out of a canon as he careened around the track.

"No headlights, either," he said, pointing to where they were painted on.

"And no windshield wipers," Mike added helpfully. His crew chief, who'd taken a shine to Kendall, showed her the layers of see-through vinyl that would be peeled off during pit stops. "Faster than wiping the windshield, and every fraction of a second counts during a pit stop."

"Really? How long does a pit stop take?" she asked, fingering the colored tab that peeled off the screen cover.

"We try to keep in the twelve-second range. Anything more than thirteen is unacceptable."

"Thirteen seconds?" She had that keen, focused look on her face that she seemed to get whenever talk turned to numbers. Dylan leaned back and watched as Mike went through the entire pit-stop routine.

"We film the crew so we can optimize efficiency."

"I can understand why. In the end, every second counts."

Mike nodded approvingly. "Dylan might tell you

different, but most races are won or lost on the pit stops." He scowled, and glared around the entire garage. "And lately, we've been losing too many."

Jack had been in the corner making calls. Dylan knew he'd given him a tough task to find a place for Kendall to stay over the race with so little notice. He also knew Jack would find something. The guy was amazing. Sure enough, by the time Kendall's eyes were beginning to glaze over from information overload, Jack walked up, looking pleased with himself.

"I've got her one of the condos." He pointed to the block of suites that overlooked the track. While some were available for rent, they were almost impossible to come by during race week.

"Nice work."

"Thanks. It's a corporate suite. They hosted a cocktail party there last night and the company president was going to stay over but he had to get back to Pittsburgh at the last minute, so it's free. Do you want me to take Kendall over?"

He thought she might feel more comfortable with him so he said, "It's okay. I'll do it."

"Keys are at the front desk. They're expecting you."

KENDALL WONDERED if she was going to wake up anytime soon.

It was Saturday night. She ought to be at home in Portland on one of her infrequent dates with Marvin or more likely watching a DVD while she ironed five blouses for the upcoming workweek.

Instead, she found herself in a golf cart being driven to a condo overlooking a racetrack by a NASCAR driver who was telling anyone who would listen that she was his new girlfriend.

She found she wasn't in a big hurry to wake up.

"These places are great. You'll love the condo. Great view."

"Great view?" Her idea of a view was rolling waves on the Pacific Ocean, the Eiffel Tower in moonlight, mountain vistas. This was a square block of windows butting onto an oval of dirt.

He must have caught her thoughts, because he grinned at her. "Great view of the track. You could watch the whole race from up there. Except you'll want to be hanging out with me."

"I will?"

"Yep. So the TV cameras get lots of pictures of us and those pictures are beamed straight into Ashlee's cockeyed brain."

"Good strategy."

"Thanks."

"I was being sarcastic."

"I'm working with what I've got. This is the best I can come up with."

She shook her head. Who was she to quibble? Her notions of strategy had won her a sideways promotion and the derision of her company's top execs.

Dylan hauled her single suitcase while she followed with her carry-on bag.

The condo was gorgeous and dominated by a wall of windows that, as he'd promised, overlooked Turn One and offered a great view of the track. She could see the luxury motor homes in the infield, where she knew Dylan would live while he was on the road. A moving crowd of people milled around, some sitting in the tiers of seats. There was room for more than 150,000 fans, Mike Nugent had told her. Billboards advertised sponsors, and logos blazed at her even from the grass beside the track.

The condo was decorated in neutral tones, which made a soothing escape from the blaze of color and action outside. A galley kitchen in white came complete with a granite breakfast bar, which opened onto a living area with a fireplace and full entertainment system.

There were two bedrooms and two bathrooms. Dylan put her stuff in the master, which boasted a queen-size bed and full en suite.

"Pretty nice," he said, wandering to the windows and looking down on the track he'd be racing on tomorrow.

"Great view," she agreed.

He turned to her. Against the background, he looked like a colossus, king of the racing world below. He was obviously itching to get back there.

"Want some down time?" he asked.

"For my imminent nervous breakdown, that would be great."

"The kitchen should be stocked. I'll give you some numbers if you need anything. I'll come back and get you for dinner."

"Dinner?"

"A casual barbecue with some of the other drivers and their families. Throw on some jeans. You'll be fine."

Jeans? She hadn't packed jeans for a corporate convention. She'd have to make do with cream linen trousers that would no doubt look completely out of place. Oh, well. She couldn't possibly look any more out of place than she'd feel.

He headed for the door, then turned. She hadn't moved. She was still standing in the middle of the cream-colored wall-to-wall carpeting in a condo overlooking Turn One of the Charlotte Speedway.

He stepped forward and squeezed her shoulder. "You're going to be fine, Kendall. You've got to trust yourself more. You're smart, decent."

She nodded, glad to be reminded that some of who she thought she was still remained. "Right." She repeated the words. "I'm smart. Decent."

He grinned at her. "And a great kisser."

CHAPTER NINE

RACE DAY. Dylan was ready. He heard the noise of the crowds, but almost as a background buzz. More, he felt the energy of all the fans, excited to be here. For many, races were part of their annual vacation. They were here for the noise, the speed, the action, to cheer their favorites and take sides in on-track rivalries. Dylan and forty-two other teams were here to make sure every one of those fans got his or her money's worth.

Kendall stood beside him taking it all in. Her eyes were big as they scanned the bleachers that seemed, from down here by the track, to stretch to the sky.

A TV reporter wandered over to do a prerace interview. Media was as big a part of this sport as the fans and the sponsors, and Dylan always tried to play nice. This one asked a lot of questions about his string of recent bad luck and wondered aloud and on camera when his streak was going to break.

"Today," he said, smiling broadly at the camera pretending, as he always did, that the lens was the face of a real fan. "Charlotte is my track." Kendall was still standing beside him and he made sure to pull her close in case Ashlee ended up watching this interview.

"Do you have any superstitions before a race, Dylan?" the reporter asked.

He thought it was a pretty stupid question, but he didn't say so. Instead, he grinned, seeing another opportunity to beam his message to his ex-wife. "I sure do. Kissing a beautiful woman is about the luckiest thing I know." And with that he turned to Kendall, who'd been doing her best to hide from the glare of the camera lights, and pulled her close. Her eyes widened and he liked the way she looked up real close. He remembered how she'd felt in his arms the other night, had a feeling she remembered, too. He took his time and kissed her until the oh-no-you-don't vibe melted beneath his lips.

With a cheer and a lot of wolf whistles from his team, he figured the lady reporter had a pretty good sound bite and some nice visuals.

"Good luck, Dylan, and thanks," she said before heading on her way.

"Good luck, Dylan," Kendall echoed. Then she added, "Drive carefully."

He slid into the car with a smile on his face and the taste of her still on his lips. She had it wrong. He always drove carefully. What he needed to do was drive fast.

People often thought that all a driver needed to do was jam his foot down hard on the accelerator and hang on. In fact, Dylan believed that a great driver was one who could read a car, one who was perceptive to small changes. Using restraint made him faster, which he'd had to learn when he first started racing. He'd trained himself to channel that impulse to win into a heightened awareness of what his car was trying to tell him, which he in turn would communicate to his crew chief, and they'd made adjustments during pit stops, fine-tuning as they went.

He took his place, midpack because of his less-than-spectacular qualifying results, and cleared his mind of everything but the machine surrounding him. *Talk to me, baby,* he told the car silently. He'd probably have spoken aloud if it weren't for the fact that a whole lot of people were listening in. He only heard two voices, that of his crew chief, sitting on top of the war wagon, and that of his spotter, up high on top of the grandstands with a bird's-eye view of the course.

He settled in and prepared to do what he did best. The race began.

There was something about five hours of nonstop concentration, where it was him and the track and the sound of the other cars that put him in a zone. Everything was so clear—well, it had to be. He didn't have a lot of time to mess around.

He listened to his spotter, used his wits and his own observations to get his car as good as he could get it. "I think we might need a pressure adjustment," he told Mike, and at the next pit stop, they made small changes and he was off again in twelve and a half seconds.

The heat inside the car climbed, but he was used to that and pretty much ignored it, sipping water as needed from the built-in water system.

There were days when nothing went right and he'd known too many of those lately. Then there were days when everything settled and it was absolutely right. He'd thought he was there yesterday, and then suddenly he wasn't. Today, he had that feeling, only stronger.

There wasn't room for much idle thought, but he knew Kendall was enjoying her first day at the track and he didn't want to be towed back in, or coast in. Not today. He didn't want to think about the possibility that he was pushing himself and his vehicle to impress a girl he barely knew, but something was giving him an extra edge today.

Maybe, he thought with an inward grin, it was that kiss. The way she had of looking at him all wide-eyed as if she'd never been kissed before. She did that every time he kissed her, and it gave him a crazy thrill. He'd kissed his share of women, and he never recalled one who looked at him afterward in quite that way. As if he'd given her a gift.

Crazy.

He licked his lips. They were dry. Hot. Like he was, coming into the final laps.

He was racing well, he knew that. His spotter was warning him of debris ahead, but he saw it and skirted the problem easily. It was so simple it was scary. He felt in control. Fast. Slick. Everything working together as it was supposed to, from the car's engine and parts all meshing and revving together to the team, working fast and efficiently.

His pit crew had been a dream team today. He wanted to reward them with the best possible time.

He told himself he was glad to finish at all, after yesterday's fiasco, but in truth he couldn't get there fast enough. He wanted more than a finish. He wanted a good finish. Not just for the placement in the race, but to show Kendall a good time.

Everything was humming and he felt good. "You're the fastest car on the track, Dy," Mike told him.

"Awesome," he yelled back. All he had to do was repeat the process every lap.

There were half a dozen cars ahead of him; if he could hold it together, he was going to have a sweet finish.

"Go high, Dylan," his spotter's voice crackled through his headset. "Looks like some trouble ahead."

What it looked like, from where Dylan sat, was that somebody'd taken a sharp left without signaling. And there went the car in the number-two spot, shooting into the grass. The third-spot holder had been hanging on, riding his draft, and he got sucked right off the track, too. Dylan was already climbing, coming into Turn Four. It was a decision moment. He could play it safe and guarantee a fourth-place finish or he could put the pedal to the metal and have some fun.

He thought of the mess they'd been having the last few weeks and fourth seemed like a dream come true.

Then he remembered that Kendall was out there watching. This was her first race ever, and he thought about how her lips had felt under his, and the way her eyes lit up when she wasn't calculating the interest on the retirement nest egg she wouldn't be needing for three or four decades.

The heck with it. He pressed his foot down and hung on.

His arms ached. He felt as if everything from his butt to his ears were on fire. Luckily, so was his driving.

He came out of Turn Four close enough to the car ahead to kiss its pretty paint job and squeak in front.

"How do you like that?" he yelled. He was sitting in third.

"How many laps?"

"Twenty-six," Mike told him. "You goin' all the way?"

Dylan laughed. He gave his trademark rebel yell. That was plenty of answer.

He didn't know when his chance would come, but he knew it would and he tried to be as patient as a man can be who smells victory and knows how easily it can be snatched.

A third-place finish was good. It was fine.

It wasn't good enough today. Not nearly.

Of course, the other two gentlemen currently holding the first and second spots felt pretty much the same way. So the three of them stuck together. Even inside the car, he could feel the energy of the crowd. There'd be discussions over beers and tailgates, in the media and in the dens and TV rooms across America about how this happened and how that other thing could have been avoided, but that would all come later. He'd be a hero or a goat depending on how he performed in the next ten or so minutes.

"I love Charlotte!" he yelled, because he felt like yelling.

"Looking good. Take it home, buddy."

And so he did. Not through any trick or maneuver, or even superior driving, though he'd like to think it was that. In these last few laps, all he could do was drive fast and hope the tires, engine, transmission and every little piece of his car held together. And that on this particular day, the only luck coming his way would be the good kind.

He edged past the vehicle in the number-two spot and felt a glorious kick of energy in his gut. He was getting tired. His arms were approaching the rubber stage, his scalp was itchy under his helmet and his eyes felt gritty—and he loved it.

At this moment, he knew, he was truly happy.

Hang on, baby, he told his car silently, the way he'd soothe a horse. *We're almost there.*

KENDALL HAD half her fist in her mouth. She couldn't take her eyes off the tiny blue-and-yellow blur that was Dylan's car. Her breathing was coming so fast and shallow she was amazed she didn't pass out from lack of oxygen.

She was on top of the war wagon, a big metal box that housed the tools and supplies for pit stops, on a chair that reminded her of a bar stool, right beside Mike Nugent. He'd given her a headset so she could hear the three-way conversation between Dylan, Mike and the spotter. Her heart was bumping crazily.

She smelled the hot dust, motor oil, hot dogs and the odor of thousands of warm bodies packed together. The fans were incredible. So colorful with their T-shirts, jackets, caps and seat cushions of their favorite drivers. They rose and cheered when the action heated up, colorful waves of bodies.

At first, she'd wanted Dylan to hang near the back of the crowd of bright cars, where it seemed quieter and he was less likely to get into any pileups. But then she watched him move forward, a little at a time, fighting his way through the pack of whizzing, colorful bullets and a crazy excitement filled her.

She'd never known anything like it. The speed, from this close, was too much for her eyes to focus on, so she saw blur after blur. For the first few laps, it felt like a sonic boom each time a car flew by, and she jumped in her seat until she became accustomed to the noise.

The crowd was crazy, the energy infectious.

"Yes!" she yelled when Mike confirmed he was in second place. "Go, Dylan," she shouted so loud she'd have embarrassed herself if everybody around her wasn't yelling a whole lot louder.

By the time he'd maneuvered his way into second she was a wreck. Her throat was sore from cheering, her palms were damp and her entire body was keyed up. When she'd learned that this race took more than five hours, with each team making about twelve pit stops, she'd imagined she'd be bored stiff. But she was having possibly the most exciting day of her life.

Now there were only minutes to go and she didn't think she could take any more. Still, her eyes stayed riveted on the contest between two front-running drivers. Dylan pulled ahead and then the other guy did, and then it was Dylan again. Suddenly there was a huge cheer and she realized the race was over.

"Who won?" she asked frantically, but there was so much noise and activity that nobody heard her.

Then Dylan's car kept going, and he was driving into the middle of the pristine lawn and making a big mess of it by turning his car in circles. Nobody seemed to mind.

That's when she knew he'd won the race.

DYLAN COULDN'T believe it.

They'd won.

In eight weeks he hadn't come closer than a tenth-place finish, but today it was as if the black cloud had blown away. A curse lifted. His bad luck routed.

Nothing was different. The team was the same, he was the same, the stock car was one of the two that had given him problems for weeks. Why today?

He gazed out at the crowd, at the TV cameras running for him, the crew and anybody who could get close, and he remembered that moment when he'd stated before a television reporter and her camera that kissing a pretty woman was his good luck superstition.

It had been a foolish piece of bravado, not said seriously, not meant to be taken that way, and yet…look what had happened.

He'd kissed Kendall Clarke and his team won a race.

Dylan wasn't a big believer in good-luck charms.

He wasn't a fool, either.

You didn't throw good luck away.

He hauled himself out of his car and looked out into a sea of people, looking for his four-leafed clover.

And there she was, beside Mike Nugent, shading her eyes with her hand and looking his way. He still had his mic, so he yelled into it to whomever was still plugged in, "Bring Kendall, will you?"

His crew chief turned and grabbed Kendall's arm and started dragging her forward. She didn't need a lot of persuading; she ran toward him. She squeaked a little bit when Dylan picked her up and swung her around, high in the air, but her eyes were dancing with excitement.

"Play along with me for the cameras, okay, honey?" he whispered.

She nodded, obviously having no clue what he was up to.

He let out a rebel yell, and then he kissed her.

Maybe she was more media savvy than he'd guessed, because this time she helped. She threw her arms around him and kissed him back.

She smelled a lot better than the inside of a stock car, tasted better than the cold beer he was looking forward to cracking. She tasted, he thought as he smiled against her lips, like luck.

Then he pulled away, keeping an arm around her waist since he knew Ashlee had to be around here somewhere, and if she wasn't she'd be seeing him on TV with his new girlfriend.

Maybe that would be enough to get the woman finally headed off on her honeymoon.

His PR guy passed him a ball cap with one of his sponsor's logos on it, and then a few microphones were stuck in his general direction.

He answered the usual questions, described some of the critical moments of the race as he remembered them, and then the gal who'd interviewed him prerace asked, "So, Dylan, introduce us to your good luck charm."

She was a nice lady, and she always tried to go easy on him, so he felt he owed her, but he hadn't expected to have to introduce Kendall on air without talking to her about it first.

"This is Kendall," he said finally.

To his astonishment, instead of directing the next question at him, the TV lady said, "Kendall, do you think you helped Dylan win the race today?"

He gave Kendall's waist a tiny squeeze, hoping she'd take the hint.

She turned his way and those cool gray eyes looked brimful of mischief. "I think every fan who cheered Dylan on today helped him win that race."

Good for her. His PR guy couldn't have scripted

anything that would have sounded better. In fact, he'd have thrown something in there about the sponsors, and as much as Dylan appreciated his sponsors, he liked that Kendall had complimented his fans.

"Do you think your kiss before the race helped?"

Kendall glanced at him again. She seemed to hesitate a second, and he knew she wasn't one for blowing her own horn. In fact, he doubted she even knew how pretty she was and how much he'd enjoyed those kisses. Then she smiled wider. "Absolutely."

"Where did you and Dylan meet?"

She hesitated and he knew she was picturing, as vividly as he was, the way she'd walked into his hotel room by mistake dressed pretty skimpily. Kendall was the kind of honest woman who would have trouble telling the whitest of white lies, so he leaned in and said, "We met through mutual friends."

He kept Kendall with him as he did post-race interviews and photos, autographs and backslapping.

"Hey, Carl," he said, as the younger driver strode up, deep-set blue eyes twinkling above a big grin.

"Nice job, Dy. I like your good-luck charm, here. Hi, Kendall."

She seemed pretty happy to see a familiar face, but then he thought his buddy had the kind of smile that made women smile back and a charm much older than his years. In the movie of Carl Edwards's life, Matt Damon would play him.

"I liked your victory kissing."

"Can't manage those backflips of yours," Dylan said.

"A man doesn't like to be predictable," he said, turning his attention to Kendall. "Anytime you want to bring me some luck…" He was enjoying himself so much a dimple appeared.

"You find your own girl to kiss," Dylan said.

"I'll try," he said and walked away with a wave.

"Somehow, I don't think he's going to have any trouble."

Dylan laughed. "You're right about that."

"Still, he sure seems like a nice guy. I'd like to help out any friend of yours."

"Don't even think about it. On the track, the only guy you kiss is me."

He looked so fierce and seemed so serious about the whole luck thing that she kept her smile stowed.

"I see. What about off the track?" She had no idea what she thought she was starting here, but the way he was gazing at her made her wish she'd kept her mouth shut. He was staring at her mouth, and the expression in his eyes could only be termed possessive. "What would it take to get an exclusive contract with those lips for the entire season?"

Kendall had never been much for flirting, but there was something about this whole NASCAR thing that was turning her into a completely different woman. So she licked those lips he was staring at. "An exclusive contract on these lips?"

"That's right."

"For a whole season?"

The heat around her wasn't coming entirely from the sun. She felt overwarm and reminded herself too late that she was toying with a man who'd been voted one of *People* magazine's hottest 50 bachelors. Her most exciting media appearance had been when her picture appeared in the company newsletter as Employee of the Month.

However, she thought, as she settled a ball cap with Dylan's picture and car number on it more firmly on her head, she was a fast learner. She sent him a saucy look. "I'll get back to you on that."

CHAPTER TEN

"I COULD KISS her myself," Jeff Geralski, his PR guy, said when Dylan introduced them after the race. "She's a natural in front of the camera. Did you see how often the kiss got broadcast and how much fun the sportscasters are having with this?"

"Yep." And the added bonus to all this coverage was knowing that it should be speeding Ashlee on her honeymoon.

"I can't believe you never brought her to a race before."

"I told you, we just met."

They were hanging out in his motor home enjoying a cold drink and the sweet feeling of victory. Jeff said to Kendall, "But you're sticking around for a while, right?"

"For a while, yes."

"Good. Excellent." He rubbed his hands. "I'm not sure if this thing has legs, but let's see what happens."

What he meant was that Dylan's luck needed to stay changed before anybody was going to believe that one kiss from one pretty woman had worked magic.

Dylan wasn't thinking about whether it was fluke or coincidence, or if Kendall was an angel sent to Earth for the sole purpose of helping him win the NASCAR NEXTEL Cup Championship. For one evening, he was kicking back and savoring the fact that his team had won.

"One race at a time, buddy," he said.

AND THEN HE WON AGAIN at Dover, finished second at Pocono and held the lead for most of the day at Michigan.

By then, he was convinced, his team was convinced, his sponsors were convinced and his fans were convinced.

Kendall Clarke was his lucky charm.

Every time he kissed Kendall before a race, he got a kind of buzz, like a shot of energy that infused him. It seemed to affect his car, too—she was running like a dream. His pit stops were short. He was driving at the top of his ability. Life was good.

Of course, there were always subtle adjustments to keep things humming, and there was one obvious correction that needed to be made.

After Michigan, he was booked for a charity golf tournament in Miami. He and Kendall and Jeff flew down together and while there he made a change that he thought Kendall, being a woman, would jump all over.

He should have remembered that Kendall rarely reacted the way he expected her to.

"What do you mean you hired me a personal shopper?" Kendall asked when he told her the news, looking deeply offended.

"Honey, you're my lucky charm. My PR guy loves you. Jeff loves that they're making us into the latest cute couple. You can't be the other half of my cute couple and wear business clothes all the time."

She looked at him, but didn't respond. She was neat as always in a trim skirt the color of compost and a blouse the color of a mushroom he wouldn't trust eating.

"I need you to wear brighter colors, things that look better on TV."

"That show more skin," she said and sniffed. Deciding that if she was supposed to look like a frivolous person, she might as well start acting like one.

Dylan's smile was slow and made her feel like an ice-cream cone that had ventured too close to the sun. "I didn't say that. NASCAR's a family sport. All I'm asking is that we find you some outfits that are more colorful, more relaxed, for the TV."

"Doesn't it bother you that from a handful of on-camera kisses, you and I are suddenly being talked about like we're a big romance?"

"Are you kidding me? If everybody in the NASCAR Series thinks you're my woman, maybe Ashlee will finally get it through her head that she is married to another man." He looked at her with a crease between his eyebrows. "Why? Does it bother you if everybody thinks we're an item?"

"Bother me? Why should it bother me?"

They were in a luxury townhome that the three of them would be sharing for the two nights they were here. Today had been crazy. They'd breakfasted with some old friends of Dylan's, Marlena and Mike from Nashville. Marlena had soft blond hair and pretty green eyes, and the way her husband looked at her, Kendall could tell they were newlyweds. After breakfast, there'd been a promotional event to attend and there'd been no question that Kendall would go along. In a very short time, Kendall had come to be as much a part of the team as the jackman or the hauler driver. It was exciting and flattering, and she was having more fun than she could have imagined. She was also more relaxed. Maybe she had needed this stress leave.

Of course, she didn't believe in luck, but so long as she was perceived as bringing it, she was having a blast. For once in her life she was in the spotlight, part of the In Crowd, and it did her battered ego good.

"I was thinking about the folks back home," Dylan said.

"I don't want to hurt your feelings, but nobody I know watches NASCAR."

He didn't look a bit offended. In fact, he chuckled. "Honey, I will offer you a money-back guarantee that everybody you know in Portland, Oregon, is going to be hearing about this. Racing news has a funny way of going mainstream."

It didn't matter to her if he thought his racing news was a bigger deal than it was. And it was sweet of him to worry about her reputation. Then, the very idea of Marvin, Mr. You're Not Exciting Enough, seeing her on TV being kissed by one of NASCAR's finest was all she needed to immediately agree to Dylan's proclamation that she needed new clothes.

"Okay," she said, imagining Marvin and pregnant Penelope seeing her living life in the fast lane. "I'll get some new clothes. But I am buying them myself."

"Kendall, you don't want to waste good money on clothes that I need you to wear."

"I won't spend a lot of money," she assured him. "I'm very good at finding treasures on the sales racks."

But he was shaking his head. "Rhoda is from around these parts, and I'm telling you right now that people talk. And talk spreads and next thing you know, everybody's saying, 'That Dylan, he sure doesn't treat his woman right. What's she doing shopping at the discount store? By the way, where's all his money?'" He threw his hands in the air like a Bible-thumping preacher. "Drugs? Gambling? Blackmail? Next thing you know, the tabloids are taking a little, itty-bitty bit of dirt and turning it into a mudslide."

She was opening and closing her mouth as if she wanted to say something so he kept on talking, figuring the longer she had to get used to the idea, the less mad she was going to be. He didn't want her buying clothes with her own money, not with her being demoted from her job, and him having more money than he knew what to do with.

"But—"

"I've got my reputation to think of, and it's not just me, it's my team. It's Mike and Jeff and the rest. You wouldn't want them being bothered by a bunch of paparazzi all because you didn't like the high-handed way I hired you a shopper who knows this town a sight bit better than you or I know it, now would you?"

"But it's chauvinistic for you to buy my clothes."

He tried another tack. "Look, you're doing me a favor. I'd really like it if you'd let me pay for a few clothes that will help you do that favor better."

Indecision was written all over her face. "It feels strange having a man buy my clothes."

"I wouldn't ask you if it wasn't important to the whole team. We've got a great streak happening, and

Jeff thinks we can get a lot of mileage out of this kissing thing. More airtime for me makes my sponsors real happy." He grimaced. "The way I've been racing lately, anything I can do to make them happy I aim to do. If I win, my whole team gets a bonus. Seems only fair you should get one, too."

"But I didn't change tires or pump gas or—"

"Doesn't matter. You definitely brought something to the team. Those kisses help us win."

It was the most ridiculous notion in the world that one kiss from her would change anything. She was an actuary. She dealt in probability and statistics, not luck. And yet, there was something intoxicating about a man like Dylan believing she, boring, mousy, not-exciting-enough-for-Marvin-Fulford Kendall Clarke could help him win a race. Today, probability and statistics were banished. Today, she would believe in luck, and maybe a little bit in magic.

She'd snuck a peek at those pictures of her and Dylan on big-screen TVs everywhere. He was right, of course; her earth-tones wardrobe was perfectly appropriate for her professional life. As the wardrobe of a NASCAR good-luck-charm kisser, her clothes definitely lacked style.

"Well, when you put it that way." She glanced at him and said, "All right. I accept."

"Thanks. Be nice to Rhoda."

"I'm always nice," she informed him.

"Oh, and buy something sexy for the dinner tomorrow night after the golf."

"But you said NASCAR is a family sport."

"It is. Tomorrow night, my ex-wife and her poor sap of a husband are joining us for dinner."

"What?"

"That's pretty much what I said when I heard. As Ashlee pointed out, they bought tickets to help support charity."

"Hah. Ruining my life is not a charity event."

He sent her the grin that transformed his tough-guy scar into a crescent moon. "So, you'll buy something sexy for tomorrow?"

"I hope your credit card has a very high limit."

"That's the go-to spirit."

The personal shopper was a five-foot-tall whirlwind of big, strawberry-blond hair, incessant gum-chewing mouth and clothing that had Kendall suspecting the woman needed to rethink her career.

Rhoda was in her mid- to late thirties, and her clothing would have looked trashy even without the excess jewelry. She jingled with big earrings, big bracelets and a big chain belt around her hips, as though she could enhance her small stature with huge accessories.

Rhoda took one look at Kendall's face and burst out laughing. "Don't worry, I get that stunned look all the time. I was brought up in a convent and ever since I got out, I crave color. I won't make you dress like me. But, honey, if you don't mind me saying so, a little color wouldn't hurt you, either. Looks better on TV. Of course, the way Dylan looks at you, I don't think he notices what you're wearing."

She waved a slim hand and long pistachio-colored fingernails flashed. Kendall stood there amazed and unable to think of a single thing to say.

Her companion laughed again. "Oh, you'll get used to me. I'm a very oral person. I talk too much. I know it. Can't help it at all." She dug a stick of gum out of a fuchsia purse hanging from a chain. "I'm giving up smoking. The gum's supposed to help, but it just makes me hungry. Chew, chew, chew and you never feel satisfied. So, what colors do you like?"

Good. Now they were getting somewhere. "I had my colors done several years ago. I'm a fall."

Rhoda made a tsking sound through her gum. "I don't believe in that stuff. What if you like black? You're never supposed to wear black because you're a fall? Besides, Dylan was very specific. He wants you in bright colors. He knows what he likes."

"But I'm the one who has to wear these clothes," she reminded the woman, trying very hard not to snarl.

"Sure you do. The trick is to find fabulous things that make everybody happy. Well? What are we waiting for? My car's out front."

As Kendall had feared, Rhoda drove the way she talked, erratically and too fast. Miraculously, they arrived at an upscale shopping district unscathed, and Rhoda led her straight into a store she'd have passed by on her own.

"I think this shop is for young people."

"What are you? The wreck of the Hatteras?"

"Hesperus," Kendall said quietly. Maybe if she kept talking in a soft voice, Rhoda would catch on and do it, too.

"Whatever."

The small woman disappeared into a swirl of colored garments and Kendall found herself following. She wasn't going to buy anything she wouldn't have purchased if alone, she reminded herself.

But there was something downright cunning about Rhoda. She'd flit and chatter and pick words at random, so Kendall was so busy trying to follow her conversation that she found herself pushed into change rooms with clothes she didn't want and then felt churlish not to try them on.

In less than an hour, she knew she'd met her match. Luckily, she was also smart enough to know that she was in the company of a genius. Clothes she would have passed by without a second glance looked much better on her than anything she'd have chosen for herself. In fact, she became quite enthusiastic as she trailed in her fashion mentor's wake. When she went so far as to ask to see a chunky, beaded turquoise necklace because she thought it matched one of the tops they'd bought, Rhoda gave her a big smile and patted her arm. "You're catching on, hon."

When they returned to the town house loaded down with bags, they got a little giggly. Everything was colorful, fun, trendy and stylish. While her dress for tomorrow's dinner wasn't sexy so much as romantic, in pale primrose with a drapey skirt and a fitted bodice, it made the most of her subtle curves.

Rhoda said, "Normally, I'd purge your closet at this point, but…" She waved her arms around the impersonal townhome. Foreseeing something like this might happen, Kendall had hidden her overnighter in her bedroom closet.

"I can at least purge that," she said, pointing to the suit Kendall was still wearing. "Then we'll have a drink to celebrate."

"But I—"

"Go on, you look so cute in your new makeup." They'd stopped for a makeover at the MAC counter and now Kendall had her own suitcase of stuff and pictures and instructions on how to use it. She had a paint-by-number face.

"What should I put on?"

"Are you going anywhere tonight?"

"I'm not sure." She'd been so focused on tomorrow, she wasn't certain if any plans had been made for tonight.

"That darling coral sundress with the lace-up sandals is good for pretty much anything."

"Okay." She crossed to the bathroom, dug through bags until she found everything, then pulled on the dress that made her think of citrus fruit. The makeup did make her look brighter and more alive, and somehow younger. Or maybe that was just the excitement of adventure, for whatever she was doing—and she didn't like to think about it too carefully or she felt queasy— this was definitely an adventure.

The only thing that was the same was her hair. She turned her head this way and that watching the brown curls glow in the bathroom light. "Should I get my hair cut?" she yelled through the door.

"No!" came the answer. And it wasn't Rhoda who answered. It was Dylan.

Okay, deep breath, quench foolish flutters. She felt girlish and flirty, and that was so unlike her that she wanted to scramble back into her safe suit. Except that Rhoda had come in and whisked it away almost as though she'd guessed this might happen.

Well, he was going to see her sometime; she might

as well get it over with. She opened the door to two staring faces.

"Oh, honey, you make me proud," said Rhoda, beaming at her as though she were her daughter trying on a bridal gown.

Dylan didn't say anything. He gave a wolf whistle.

Kendall wasn't a troll. She got whistled at by the usual construction guys and drunks on street corners, but she'd never, ever received a wolf whistle from an actual red-blooded, hot, womanizing wolf.

So maybe a little shopping once in a while wasn't such a bad thing.

CHAPTER ELEVEN

"WANT TO COME with me later when I'm putting suntan lotion on some gals in bikinis?" Dylan asked.

They were back in Florida, getting ready for the next race in Daytona. She was starting to get used to the routine, the village of motor homes where she and Dylan stayed for a few days over the race, where she appeared in public as his girlfriend with the lucky lips while in private they'd become friends. They were sharing a quick soda before he headed off to the track.

At the expression on her face, he grinned. "I swear it wasn't my idea. It's an ad for one of my sponsors and I would take it as a real favor if you would come with me."

"You don't want to be alone with all those barely dressed models?"

He shook his head. "Just come with me."

She knew now that he liked having her around some-times as a buffer between him and the outside world, sometimes as his Sorry I'm Taken sign. "Okay."

"Thanks. I'm heading down to the garage. See you after practice. We'll do the ad, then be back here for dinner?"

"Sure." They often ended up having barbecues or

simply hanging out with other drivers, their wives and families. She always enjoyed watching Dylan with the kids. He probably spent more time with the youngsters than he did with the adults.

They were all on the road together so much that friendships formed. It was like a club or an extended family, and Kendall found herself becoming an accepted member of the club. No one questioned whether she was really Dylan's girlfriend, and she couldn't exactly explain the situation, so she kept up the pretense and was grateful to have the other wives and girlfriends to talk to.

These were the women who understood this world and who could help her handle media or aggressive fans and, whether they realized it or not, they gave her insight into what made a driver tick, something she was desperately trying to figure out.

Sometimes she would daydream that she really did belong, but that was crazy thinking, so she'd mentally slap herself even as she hoped Dylan's winning streak continued so she had a reason to stay.

Her twelve weeks of stress leave were halfway over. As a cure for stress, joining the NASCAR circuit probably wasn't the most common prescription, but if the idea of stress leave was to get her mind off her job and the messy love triangle of her, Marvin and Penelope, then NASCAR had cured her.

She barely thought of Marvin except with mild distaste and she didn't think of her job at all. In six weeks she had to report to her new position as the assistant branch manager of a storefront insurance agency in Aurora. Her interim position as Dylan's good-luck charm was vastly more amusing. And with a much better wardrobe.

She'd become comfortable in her new clothes and found that she liked the sunny colors and casual outfits. Her emergency calls to Rhoda were down to one a week, tops, as she gained confidence in her own choices.

Dylan's luck was holding, as was the myth of the cute couple they made.

"Dylan?" she said, just before he stepped out.

"Uh-huh?" He paused in the act of shoving one of his endless ball caps on his head.

"Is Ashlee going to be at the race?"

"She has a condo here. What do you think?"

She rolled her eyes and immediately replanned what she'd wear tomorrow. She had no idea what Dylan's ex thought she was up to. Their so-called—and never-ending—honeymoon had mostly been spent, as far as Kendall could tell, in popping down to Daytona Beach, where Ashlee's family owned a condo, every time Dylan was anywhere near the place. The charity golf tournament dinner had been a nightmare as Dylan held Kendall against him like a shield. Ashlee had alternately pouted at, flirted with and charmed Dylan, while blowing hot and cold on her husband until Kendall ended up with a tension headache.

Not even the prettiest dress she'd ever owned and a couple of dreamy slow dances with Dylan had saved the evening from becoming a painful memory.

SHE WATCHED Dylan run his morning practice and only bit through one fingernail.

When he pulled in, he climbed out the window, the same way he'd entered the car. She still wasn't used to cars with no doors, stick-on decals for headlights or peel-off wrap instead of windshield wipers. It was weird.

Dylan walked up to Mike Nugent and they talked technical, so the few words she caught made no sense. However, Mike soon had a couple of the guys on the team fiddling with the engine while Dylan got ready for qualifying.

She wasn't sure if he'd kiss her, since it was, first, a qualifier and, second, no media were near. He seemed to hesitate. She felt the eyes of the entire crew on them, and she thought that was what made him move toward her and smack her soundly on the lips. The feeling of relief from the crew was palpable. Amazing. They actually believed the flawed kiss-equals-good-luck equation.

Dylan had the fifth fastest time of the forty-three drivers who'd compete tomorrow. That put him in the front group and he seemed pretty jazzed about that. "You always bring me good luck," he said. "Thanks."

She was ready to leave the dirt and oil smells and the noise of the racetrack, but of course their day wasn't over.

Jack appeared and bundled Dylan and her into a limo. They drove to where one of Dylan's sponsors, a suntan lotion, had organized the photo shoot for an ad. Dylan was placed in front of one of his cars, with half a dozen models all in bikinis. Dylan's job was to spread suntan lotion on the women.

He didn't seem to mind the extra time he was putting in at the office at all.

After she'd watched him slather a ridiculous amount of lotion on a ridiculous amount of nubile skin, they were finally allowed to leave. She saw one of the girls whisper in his ear, an obvious invitation. Dylan pulled his I'm-too-sexy-for-my-car act and pocketed a slip of paper the model handed him.

Oh, great.

"I hope I didn't spoil your fun," she said, when they were loaded back in the limo.

"Not at all. Those girls wanted to go party, but I explained you and I already had plans."

"They were jailbait, anyway." She wanted to get a few things straight, but not with Jack listening to every word. Besides, she didn't get a chance. Dylan's cell phone went off.

She knew it was Ashlee the minute he started talking. She spent most of the limo ride talking to Jack and resisting the urge to bash Dylan with the bottle of suntan lotion she'd been given.

ASHLEE AND HARRISON showed up at the race the next day, as Kendall had known they would, but Ashlee was surprisingly low-key for once. Kendall wore a pretty apricot-colored gauzy sundress and put extra effort into kissing Dylan both before and especially after he placed third.

Amazingly, the ex-wife didn't even try to get the four of them out for dinner together or some other horrendous double date, perhaps because she sensed Kendall would make up an excuse not to go.

She was congratulating herself on helping Dylan ease out of his ex-wife's clutches when he told her he'd be staying an extra day in Daytona Beach. Dylan had agreed to visit the children's ward of a local hospital. The visit wasn't on his schedule, she knew, since she kept a copy of his itinerary on her laptop computer. It helped her feel organized and gave some structure to her life to look ahead at events she'd take part in.

The next morning, they set off in a car he'd borrowed from a local dealership. She wondered if his driving it for a day would up the sticker price. It was nice, driving alone with Dylan. There was no Jack from marketing, no Jeff from PR; it was only the two of them, which was rare, she realized. Then she made the mistake of glancing at the speedometer.

"I've never been in Florida before this year," she said, for something to say, to keep her mind off the fact that he was driving much too fast in her opinion. "It's beautiful."

He shot her a glance and she bit her tongue to prevent herself from snapping at him to keep his eyes on the road. "The tourism people will be real happy to hear that."

Not only did his eyes move from what they should be doing, but now his hand joined in, leaving the steering wheel to land on her knee, warm and heavy. His fingers toyed with the hem of her flowered summer dress and moved against her skin. He did that sometimes, touched her in a way that was both friendly and something more. However, she was starting to see through his tricks, to understand that he used his warmth and undeniable charm for his own ends. "You're trying to distract me," she said.

"From what?" He sounded all innocent, but the scar was changing shape, from an *L* to a *C,* always a sign that he was amused and trying not to show it.

"From the fact that you're doing sixty-four in a fifty-five-mile zone."

"You know how fast I was going when I won at Talladega?"

She started to remind him that this wasn't a controlled racetrack but her insatiable love of numbers got in the way. "How fast?"

"Average speed was one-eighty-four miles an hour and change."

She glanced at the speedometer again. "I can't even imagine how fast that is. What's it like?"

He played with the hem of her dress absently while he thought, and she tried to ignore the sensations of warmth fluttering through her. "When you go that fast, the noise of the tires on the road surface are like a high-pitched whine. The g-force sucks you into the seat and it's hot. Like sitting on top of a furnace."

"Wow."

"There's no room to think of anything. I'm working with the car. Reading its signals, talking to Mike. Working our strategy."

"Is it noisy?" She thought about how she'd felt the physical impact of all that noise the first time she'd seen a race. The fans, the cars, the booming microphones.

"I don't notice the noise. Sometimes I get out of the car and hear all those fans yelling, and I'm a little bit surprised. I'd almost forgotten they were there."

"That's some focus."

He nodded, not speaking.

Another couple of miles rolled by. "Why do you do it?" she asked suddenly.

"Do what? Tease you? Because you're so uptight, it's the—"

"No. Not that. Racing. Why do you race?"

He glanced over. "You really want to know?"

"Yes."

"Is this going to end up in you telling me that I'm eleven point four times more likely to be involved in a car crash than a person who stays in their basement watching televised bowling? Because I have to tell you, that is getting old."

"No, I'm—"

"Has it occurred to you that you are eleven point four times more likely to get into trouble hanging around with me than if you'd gone home to your regular life?"

"Oh, yes. That has definitely occurred to me." The funny thing was that she couldn't seem to care. Of course, her time with Dylan was short. She was on holiday from her own life, and like any holiday, it would end, hopefully with no regrets and some pleasant memories.

The wind whipped through her hair and she tipped her face up to the sun. Dylan turned up the CD player for a song he liked. The music was too loud and the increased volume wasn't making her change her mind about country music, but it kept right on wailing whether she minded or not.

"You want to know why I race," he said at last, shouting above the music.

"Yes." She hadn't thought he'd answer and was content to let it go, but she was curious as to what he'd say.

"I like the rush. I like the speed. I like the challenge."

"And you like the attention from the fans," she added.

He shot her a crooked grin. "I didn't say that."

She wrinkled her nose in thought, recalling the races she'd seen so far. "What about the crowds, the women, the...adulation?"

He looked right at her. "The women are nice. Definitely."

Even though she wasn't in the league of some of the women she'd seen hanging around the drivers, she appreciated the flattery. It wasn't as though she'd received so much of it in her life that it was tedious.

However, watching him take numbers from models and chat to his ex was starting to get on her nerves.

She reached forward and turned down the music. "Uh-oh," he said.

"I wanted to...um...talk about something."

"The kissing thing?"

Persistence, she reminded herself. In interpersonal communication, persistence was often required to ensure her message was correctly received. "Well, that's sort of what I wanted to talk to you about."

"You didn't like the kiss yesterday? Or you were disappointed we only came in third? Honey, I have to tell you, the luck is holding. I can't win every race, but our team is doing better than we've done all season. You really are our lucky charm."

"You don't seriously believe that."

"I believe the results speak for themselves."

"The thing is, I thought our time together would end sooner, that the good-luck thing wouldn't hold up."

All amusement was gone from his face. She even felt the car slow as though the gravity of the situation was communicating itself to the engine. "What are you saying?"

"Everyone thinks I'm really your girlfriend."

"Right. Which was our plan. So?"

"Maybe this is crazy. I know I'm only your pretend girlfriend, but I'd appreciate fidelity."

"I'm not sure I follow you, honey. All we do is a little kissing."

She felt foolish but she was a woman of strong morals, and even in a pretend relationship it was important for her to believe in her man. "I know. But if you are seen with other women, it makes me look foolish."

"So now you're asking for an exclusive on my lips."

She gaped at him and caught the crinkle around his eyes that told her he was teasing her again.

"Oh, just forget I ever spoke," she snapped and turned up the volume on the car's CD player.

With a click the music was silenced completely, and the car made a neat little *S*. Suddenly they were pulled over into a picnic area.

Dylan opened his door and got out, strolling over to check out the graffiti on a picnic table. She got out and stretched her back, then walked over to join him.

"You want a drink?" he asked, heading for a soda machine.

"Thanks. Sparkling water or juice if there is any."

He fed coins into the machine and came over with a couple of cans. Passed her one.

Her stomach felt a little jumpy and she wondered if the greatest adventure of her life was about to end. She probably should have kept her mouth shut, but she knew she couldn't do that. She needed to be honest and she needed to keep her dignity, whatever the cost.

"Here's the thing," he said, looking at the table rather

than at her. "I asked you to help me out of a jam and you did. I asked you to act like you were crazy about me and you did that, too."

She nodded.

"Now, we've worked so hard to convince Ashlee that we're an item, I'd be crazy to go out with other women, right?"

"I suppose. If she was going to find out."

"Oh, she'd find out. You don't know Ashlee. She still has friends who are married to or girlfriends of the guys. They fill her in on everything."

"I saw you take that model's phone number, after the ad shoot."

He made an embarrassed face. "It was reflex. I didn't want to hurt her feelings, so I took it. You didn't see me throw the paper away later."

"No. But the point is you took it, which made me feel slighted."

"Honey, I'm sorry. I wasn't going to phone that girl, and there was nowhere to put that paper if I gave it back to her."

"There was quite a bit of room in her bra cup. At least a *D*'s worth."

"I should have thought about your feelings. You're right. But believe me, I'm not going to date anyone while you're around."

"You won't date anyone else so that Ashlee doesn't find out?" And her confidence was at an all-time high.

"No. That's one reason. I also heard what you said. You don't want to share."

"Right."

"I respect that. I don't want to share you, either."

"You don't?"

He gazed at her over his drink can, eyes narrowed against the sun.

She felt a huge sense of relief, but he didn't seem to be having the same reaction to their little talk. In fact, she realized when he finished drinking that he wasn't done talking.

"I didn't make any promises, Kendall, and I won't be making any."

"Promises?" What promises?

"You're a nice woman. You also seem like the kind who wants to settle down and have a few kids in the near future so you can calculate the odds that they get into med school or Yale, or that they'll break their arms if they take up softball. Am I right?"

She decided to ignore his animadversions on her professional background. "I do plan to get married someday and hope to raise a family. Yes."

"Just so we're both clear on that, I am not your guy."

She was so surprised she choked on her juice, and then got caught between a laugh and a cough so that it gurgled up into her nose and burned. "Ow, ow," she cried, digging in her bag for a tissue.

He slapped her on the back, nearly knocking her out. "You okay?"

She nodded and waved him back. When she had blown her nose and composed herself, she stared at him.

"You think I would want to marry you?"

He blinked at her as though she'd asked the stupidest question he'd ever heard. "I'd prefer you didn't, but just for the record what is so hysterically funny about the idea?"

She smiled at him, a big, happy sunbeam of a smile that showed all her teeth. "You are exactly what I need right now and I will always be grateful that you told me to jump into your car in Charlotte. I love being your good-luck charm and I can probably get used to the noise and the smell of the racetrack, given time, but there's no long-term for us. There couldn't be."

"Right. Right. That's what I'm saying." He kicked some gravel around with his feet. "I know why I think that, but why do you?"

She gaped at him. "Dylan, you would be a terrible husband and father." Realizing how rude that sounded, she hastily added, "For me, I mean. You're so restless and on the road so much. I'm looking for a family man."

"So, I'm an unacceptable risk as a husband and father, that's what you're saying?"

Glad he understood her so well, she said, "Yes."

"You've calculated it all out with a calculator and a spreadsheet. I'm good enough for a few kisses and some laughs."

"Exactly. A monogamous pretend relationship."

"Well, honey, it looks like we've got a deal, because we both want the same thing, and we're both agreed I'd make a lousy dad."

There was a note of bitterness that broke through his cheerful tone and caused her brow to furrow. Something was going on here that she didn't understand. "I'm sure you'd make a wonderful father." She thought of all the times he'd spent an extra minute with one of his younger fans, and how all the kids of the other drivers treated him like a favorite big brother. He always had time to kick a football around or joke or talk sports. "I didn't mean—"

He tossed his drink can into the recycling container and started walking back to his car. "Let's go."

As they continued the drive, she was desperate to change the subject. "How are you going to entertain a bunch of sick kids? Some of whom, I hate to tell you, might not be racing fans."

"I have hidden talents, my friend."

"Do you?"

"I can make an entire menagerie of balloon animals. Poodles, lions, water buffalo, you name it."

"Really?" She was delighted, especially since he'd obviously decided to let his weird mood go. Dylan— the easygoing, laid-back, fun guy—had returned. "What a great talent to have."

She loved this part of the world, the vast sandy beaches, so different from the rugged Oregon coastline; the Atlantic; the hot weather. She loved having time alone with Dylan and, as awkward as the conversation had been, she was glad they'd talked about the importance of fidelity in their fake relationship.

"So, who booked you for this?"

There was a pause. "Ashlee."

So much for fidelity. "Ashlee? You've barely got any time in your schedule and you're doing this for Ashlee?"

"I am doing it for some kids who could use a laugh," he reminded her.

"And your clingy ex-wife isn't going to be anywhere near, right?"

"Of course she'll be there. She's the one who set this up."

CHAPTER TWELVE

DYLAN ANSWERED questions that were fired at him faster than ones at any media scrum she'd ever seen. A dozen or so kids were assembled in the ward, and whether or not they knew who Dylan was, they seemed pretty excited.

"What's the fastest you ever drove?"

"About two hundred miles an hour."

"Do you have any kids?"

"No."

"Are you a millionaire?" Giggles.

"Yep."

"Is that your girlfriend?"

Dylan raised his head and caught sight of Kendall standing in the doorway. A beat passed. There were no media here, no Ashlee or crowds of fans for whom the deception mattered. "Yep," he said again, and dropped his gaze back to the group of kids.

"What's her name?"

"Kendall."

This was the guy who'd told her he'd be a terrible father?

"Where's Ashlee?" Kendall asked him when there was a short pause.

"I don't know. She's supposed to be here, with the balloons."

"Got it. Keep talking. Tell them some of your charming anecdotes. I'll be right back."

He had a bag of ball caps that he'd planned to sign and give out at the end of the show, but Kendall handed it to him now, figuring a change in the program would give her more time to find balloons.

She ran out, cursing Ashlee all the way to the car. She asked for help in a bakery that specialized in kids' birthday cakes and was directed to a strip mall to find the right kind of balloons for twisting into animals. Then she got lost trying to find the strip mall.

Kendall came dangerously close to breaking the speed limit on her way back to the hospital.

As soon as she returned with the balloons to the fifth-floor children's ward, she felt a buzz in the air. There was a lot of noise and laughter coming from the open doorway.

When she peeked in the doorway she saw Dylan, sitting on a table and surrounded by kids. Kids on crutches, in wheelchairs, kids dragging IV poles and oxygen tanks. No matter how pale, or thin, they were all laughing. Many of them held balloon animals, like the one Dylan was currently fashioning.

She let out a shaky breath and slid quietly into the room, putting down the bag of balloons. Ashlee was there, standing unnecessarily close to Dylan, handing him balloons.

She wanted to be angry, but Ashlee actually looked as if she cared about these kids and, whatever her motive, it was a good thing. Jeff would love this, she thought.

What a great photo op. But Jeff wasn't here. The media weren't here. It was just Dylan and a bunch of kids.

Dylan talked while he twisted balloons into what she thought was a giraffe. The way he talked to the shy young girl who was waiting for her giraffe made Kendall's heart flip over. She had long blond hair, a pretty face and a clear breathing tube connected to a portable oxygen tank. She wore jeans and a T-shirt that announced a fun run in aid of cystic fibrosis funding.

Deciding that she wasn't needed, and she'd rather drink hospital machine coffee than hang around watching Ashlee drool on Dylan, she headed back to a seating area she'd noted when they first came in. To her surprise, she found Harrison sitting stiffly in one of the chairs flipping through an ancient *Reader's Digest*. He was the only person there.

"Harrison," she said.

He glanced up, nodded, then put down his magazine. "Kendall. I thought you'd be helping with the balloons."

"I think Dylan's getting plenty of help. Ashlee is sitting so close to him you'd think he was a ventriloquist and she was his dummy," she snapped, and then gasped at her own rudeness. "I'm sorry. I shouldn't have said that."

"Ashlee is never subtle," Harrison said. As if that were breaking news.

She nodded.

He picked up a well-thumbed and unsanitary-looking magazine from the stack and then put it down again. He turned to her. "You're probably wondering why I let her treat me this way."

In fact, she'd been wondering that since their wedding day when she first met the three of them. Since he'd opened the door to discussing his private life, she was happy to walk through it.

"Why do you?" she asked, sitting beside him on a brown vinyl chair.

"I love her," he said simply.

Somehow, coming from this pompous, too-rich guy, the words sounded more sincere than anything else he'd ever said in her company.

What could she say? Ashlee spent a lot more time trying to talk Dylan into getting back together than she did basking in the love of her new husband. She glanced at him uncertainly.

"She loves me, too," he said. Okay, there was the blind ego she'd come to know and not love. He glanced her way and his lips tilted as though he'd read her mind. "She really does love me. She simply hasn't accepted it yet."

"When do you see her doing that?"

"A lot depends on you."

"Me?" Shock had her squeaking out the word like a very inquisitive mouse.

"Why do you think Ashlee keeps wanting to do these horrendous double dates?"

"I was thinking it was some kind of torture ritual."

He smiled slightly and shook his head. "She's watching you. Ashlee is a…complicated woman. Our background, the three of us, it's complicated, too. Think about it." Here he allowed himself another small, amused smile. "She was the prettiest girl in the town. In the county. I was in love with her from the second I saw her in high school. I mean real, love-at-first-sight stuff."

"Wow. And you waited all this time?" And for what, she wondered, but a big dose of heartache.

"Ashlee and Dylan were the golden couple growing up. High school prom king and queen, you know the types."

Oh, she did. She'd watched those types from afar all her life.

He took a breath and she saw in that moment the pain of heartbreak he'd endured, that young success story who could get everything he wanted but the girl he loved. "So I got on with my life. Went to Harvard, learned some skills that I hope will keep our factory competitive and our labor force working for the next couple of decades." He glanced at her.

"You didn't marry a nice MBA or law grad?"

"No. I kept waiting, hoping Ash would come to her senses. I could see they were all wrong for each other."

"And yet Dylan married Daisy." She blinked, realizing she'd let her private name slip. "I mean, Ashlee."

But Harrison was chuckling. "Daisy as in Gatsby's Daisy? Not a bad parallel. I hope I end up better than Gatsby, though."

"I hope so, too," she said, thinking more than just Ashlee's happiness was at stake. "Can't you take Ashlee away from here? Spending so much time hanging around her ex-husband can't be a good idea."

"I could, of course, find an excuse to take her away from Dylan, but then she's never going to realize that she's over him. Has been over him for years. She not only loves me, but she needs me. I give her stability and—" he sent Kendall a swift, rueful glance "—she gives me excitement."

He might be right that Ashlee was in love with him. Kendall had seen no evidence of it at all, however. Also, she could see what Harrison obviously couldn't. Put the two men together and Dylan, with his easy charm and slight air of danger, was by far the more interesting.

Again, it seemed as though Harrison read her thoughts. "I don't pretend to be an exciting man like Dy. I don't even want to be. If you weren't around, I'd be dragging Ashlee home, but Ash isn't as dumb as she appears. I think she's finally starting to realize that you and Dylan have something special and it's letting her accept the possibility that she and I have something special."

"But she's hooked on that reading from her astrologer telling her that she's destined to end up with a man from her past."

He sighed heavily. "Does no one ever consider the possibility that I am a man from her past?"

"It doesn't matter what anyone else thinks. It only matters what Ashlee thinks," she reminded him.

"Right. And she's starting to think that maybe Dylan's finally found someone who is right for him. When she gives up the idea of getting back together with him, she'll see what's under her nose."

"How can you live like this?" she burst out.

He picked up an ancient *Golf Magazine* and straightened it on top of an old *National Geographic.* "I miscalculated. I made the foolish mistake of thinking that Ashlee looked on marriage the way most of us do—as a permanent arrangement, not an excuse for a party."

"I'm sure she wants her marriage to last," Kendall said, more as a sympathetic gesture than that she really thought anything of the kind.

"I'm sure she does, too. And when she sees how happy you and Dylan are, she's going to forget about that astrologer. Kendall, I'm counting on you."

"I'm not what you think I am," she said suddenly, because in the face of such raw honesty she found she couldn't lie to Harrison.

"You don't know what I think you are, so that is a ridiculous statement."

"What I'm trying to say is—"

"Don't forget I've known Dylan as long as I've known Ashlee. He may hate my guts, but it doesn't stop me from understanding him in a way I doubt he understands himself." He looked at her fully. "He's as terrified of commitment as Ashlee is. Don't run away. He'll do his best to drive you away, but don't go. I don't mean to be dramatic, but I think all our happiness depends on you."

"Our entire relationship is a pretense," she snapped, unable to stop the words she'd promised not to utter. "The whole thing's an act to make Ashlee leave him alone."

"Sure it is," said Harrison with a knowing arch of the eyebrow that made her want to smack him.

She walked to the vending machine and got herself a coffee. She offered Harrison one, but he simply looked at her as if she was out of her mind for drinking that stuff. But then he hadn't run all around a strange town in a panicky search for balloons that turned out not to be needed.

All our happiness depends on you, Harrison had said.

She returned to her chair and sat down. She sipped her coffee.

"Okay," she said. "This is none of my business." It was also risky to give personal advice to a man she barely knew, and she didn't usually take emotional risks. Hanging around with Dylan was making her as crazy as he was. "But you're making it too easy for Ashlee."

He looked at her strangely. "I beg your pardon?"

"I know. This is pushy and I am never pushy, but I can't seem to help myself."

"You've been spending too much time with Dylan."

She smiled at the way they both assumed Dylan was responsible for her changing. "Probably."

"Go on. I suppose I'm desperate enough to take advice from someone who is as hopelessly in love with Dylan as I am with Ashlee."

She blinked and experienced an odd sensation, as though she were about to pass out. "I'm not hopelessly..." She couldn't finish the sentence because she'd always tried to tell the truth and even as she formed the words to deny his charge, she realized he was right. She was in love with Dylan. And hopeless didn't begin to describe it.

His face softened and he leaned over to touch her shoulder. "Sorry. Maybe it's not hopeless. What do I know? I should have known it was hopeless when I married Ashlee."

"No. Your marriage wasn't a mistake." She pushed thoughts of her own romantic troubles aside. "Ashlee is confused, that's all. She left Dylan once and for good reason. You're right. Those two are all wrong for each other. They're too alike. Anyone can see—"

"You can see it and I can see it, but we aren't exactly objective observers."

"Right." She sighed.

"But I'll try anything. What do you think I should do?"

She sipped her coffee again. "What Ashlee does so well. Play hard to get."

"Excuse me, but I already graduated from high school."

"Maybe, but this crazy love-hate triangle with the three of you sure hasn't."

"And how do you suggest I play hard to get with my own wife?"

"Stop coming with her when she follows Dylan around. It can't be any fun."

"Having my liver chewed by cockroaches would be more fun."

"Exactly."

"But…I don't know. If I'm not there she might do something crazy."

"I know. She might convince him to get back together."

"It's a big risk."

"For both of us."

He sat back. Drummed his fingers on the knee of his impeccable trousers. "I've got business at home that can't wait. I shouldn't be hanging around like this as it is."

He stood, paused there another moment, and then, with a sudden nod, as though he'd just made up his mind about something, started walking down the hall in the direction of the balloon party with such determination in his stride that she had to jog to catch up.

The balloon animals were all done, and Ashlee and Dylan were spending one-on-one time with a couple of the kids. Ashlee had a little girl about two sitting in her lap, playing with her hair. There were bandages on the girl's legs.

Dylan was talking quietly to a couple of older boys, while a nurse listened in.

"Ashlee," Harrison said, putting his head into the room. "I'm heading back. Are you coming with me, or do you want to catch up later?"

His wife glanced up in surprise, as did Dylan. This was the first tiny test. Would Ashlee choose Dylan or Harrison?

She wavered, and then looked into the sleepy face of the child still playing with her hair. "I'll come later," she whispered.

Harrison sent Kendall a thanks-for-nothing glance and walked away.

Dylan didn't appear any more pleased, but after about fifteen minutes, when the child in her lap was sound asleep, Ashlee and one of the nurses left to put the sleeping child into her crib.

Ashlee returned a few minutes later and said, "Well, I'd better be on my way. I'll see you two soon."

"Don't you want a ride back?"

She hesitated. "No. I'll get a cab." With a wave, she was gone.

Kendall let out a breath of relief. Harrison hadn't won this round, but he hadn't lost it, either. It was more of a draw.

"Ready?" Dylan said, when even the eager young boys had wandered off to watch TV.

She looked at him, at that tough, wonderful face. Harrison had been so right. She'd gone and fallen in love with Dylan. Dangerous to her heart, terrible risk as a future mate, the man she wanted to spend her life with: Dylan.

Ready? Of course she wasn't ready.

Kendall had never been a woman who went after the stars. She calculated the odds and made sure her goals stayed well within reach.

Why?

Why did she sell herself so short?

More to the point, her strategy hadn't worked out very well. Her very achievable fiancé was a rat and the company she'd spent all her working life with hadn't stood by her the minute she hit a patch of trouble.

Loving Dylan was a risk. Not a risk she could afford, since she didn't believe in taking unnecessary chances. And yet, she didn't believe in the concept of luck, either, and here she was a walking, talking rabbit's foot. A personal four-leaf clover.

Maybe, she thought, as she stood there, accepting the truth that she'd fallen in love with Dylan, maybe some risks were worth taking. A new and potent sense of her own worth percolated through her system. She'd always been content to shoot for the horizon rather than the stars. She'd always assumed it was her personality; now she wondered if she'd simply been too scared to reach beyond her comfort zone.

Since she'd been flung so far out of her comfort zone, it was like viewing her life from space. She'd had more fun than ever before. She was respected—okay, wished upon—and valued.

As insight into her life grew, so did the knowledge that she saw in the devil-may-care race car driver a man who was in some ways as fundamentally conservative as she was.

Why?

Why did a man who so obviously loved kids and who was so comfortable with the other drivers' families warn her away from himself as a long-term risk? It was easy to believe that he'd tried to warn her away because she wasn't pretty enough or hot enough or woman enough, but somehow her self-esteem had grown in the short time she'd been with Dylan and she saw that he sincerely did believe he was somehow lacking.

Again, why?

It was no longer idle speculation. She really wanted to know, because now that she realized she loved him, Kendall—the new and improved Kendall—wasn't about to let him go without a fight.

CHAPTER THIRTEEN

KENDALL WASN'T sure where she was. The usual compound of motor homes had become so familiar around her that sometimes she forgot where they were geographically.

She and Dylan had fallen into the routine of racing couples: Thursday to Sunday at whatever track the schedule required. After the race, they'd fly back to Dylan's home base. He owned a house about an hour's drive outside Charlotte, and that was home for half a week unless he had sponsor events, promotions or appearances of various kinds. They'd spend Sunday night to Wednesday at home and then start the whole thing back up again.

If she hadn't become so valuable to Dylan, she'd feel like a freeloader, but Kendall knew she'd become important to him. Sadly, not in the will-you-take-this-woman-to-be-your-lawfully-wedded-wife manner, but she knew he cared. They lived as roommates except when the camera was on them and the pre- and postrace kissing happened. Those were the moments that she lived for. In the meantime, she made his life easier in ways she doubted he even noticed and tried not to count the weeks that were ticking away until this amazing adventure was over and she started her new job.

She was out taking a walk, leaving Dylan on one of his endless business calls, when it finally occurred to her.

"New Hampshire," she said aloud, remembering where they were. New Hampshire, and her twelve weeks were almost gone. The race schedule to her was a countdown of her time with Dylan. They never spoke of it, but she sometimes wondered if he'd ask her to stay beyond the three months of her leave, and what she'd say if he asked.

Indianapolis. That's where she'd be saying goodbye. When summer ended, so did her leave. She was expected in Aurora when the new branch office opened.

Even though she sometimes toyed with the idea of staying on if he asked her to and thumbing her nose at the company she'd been with for eight years, she knew she wouldn't do it. Not unless Dylan wanted her for more than luck.

She was puzzled and determined to find out why a man who was so obviously family-oriented was pushing away a woman who might just be the best thing that had ever happened to him. She smiled a little at her own conceit, kind of liking the powerful feeling it gave her.

A voice pulled her out of her reverie. "Hey, did I do something to offend you? You were going to walk right past me."

She glanced up. Carl Edwards was strolling toward her in a sweat-stained T-shirt and athletic shorts, a half-empty water bottle in his hand. "Carl. I'm so sorry. My mind was miles away. I didn't see you."

"Not the most flattering greeting I ever got," he said, falling into step with her. "And there I was thinking that smile of yours was for me."

"No. I was thinking of Dylan."

Carl clapped his hands over his heart and pretended to fall over. "You're killing me, here."

She laughed, feeling suddenly lighter and more hopeful about the future. "Oh, stop it." Then she realized that this man probably knew Dylan as well as anyone around here. He certainly understood the mentality of a driver. So she put a hand on his arm. "Can I ask you something?"

"Sure."

"What does a NASCAR driver look for in a woman?"

"Shoot. I thought you were going to ask me something easy, like how to calculate the g-force based on wind velocity and metal mass of a car's chassis." She sent him a reproving look from under her lashes and he unleashed that megawatt grin on her. "Okay, seriously, are we talking drivers in general or one tough ol' boy in particular?"

"I'm hoping understanding the general will help with the particular."

Carl was silent for a while, his head tilted back as though stargazing, but she thought he was taking her question seriously enough to think about his answer. "I'm guessing that what we all look for deep down is a woman we can be our true selves with. Somebody we can relax with." He took a drink from his water bottle and continued.

"They have to be tolerant. A woman needs to understand the focus. The harder I work, the better I do. This sport will take as much devotion as I have to give."

She nodded silently. She'd seen that focus.

"There's forty to a hundred people dedicated to working for me. I don't want to let them down, and if I'm out at the movies every night with my girlfriend, it's not going to work."

"So, you're looking for someone who supports you and believes in you?" I can do that, she thought. She was tolerant of the time Dylan gave to his sport and the people who counted on him. She admired that quality in him. She certainly believed he was relaxed when she was around. Damn it, she was perfect.

"I'm looking for a strong woman who's honest." He thought a little more. She liked the way he answered her question so seriously, but then she'd known he would. "You've seen what it's like. The fans, the media, the speed. It can get to you pretty fast, maybe go to your head a little bit if you're not careful. The best women are the ones who are grounded, who are a hundred percent committed to their families. I guess that's what we're all looking for."

Okay, so maybe she wasn't as strong as she could be, and how honest was it to pretend to be the girlfriend of the man you were in love with? But she absolutely felt committed to the idea of Dylan and family. If she wasn't perfect for him, she was very, very close.

"You seem to be enjoying being a bachelor pretty well."

Carl treated her to that grin again. "I didn't say right away, but that's what I'm looking for. Now Dylan, he's a lot older than me. He should be looking a lot harder."

"Yes," she said sadly. "He should."

"You know what I think, Kendall?"

"What?"

"I think a man like Dylan is pretty good at hiding

what he doesn't want the world to see. A good woman might have to push a little bit to get what she wants."

"Is that a fact?"

"Yes, ma'am. That is a fact."

On impulse, she leaned up and kissed his cheek. "You're a good man. Thanks."

When she turned back toward Dylan's trailer, she noticed a man sitting on his front step, watching her. All her senses came alert as they always did when that particular man looked at her. She walked closer. "I thought you were still on the phone."

"I got off in time to see you kissing another man," he said, his voice sounding possessive rather than jealous. Figured.

"I only kissed his cheek. Hardly any luck gets passed along that way."

"I'm glad to hear it." He yawned. "Why were you kissing him if it's not too personal?"

Hallelujah. Maybe he was a tiny bit jealous after all. Her mood rose.

"We were talking about family," she said.

"Hmm." He tipped a can of soda to his lips. She sank down beside him and when he offered, took it from him and helped herself to a sip.

"You want one?"

"No, thanks." It had to be fate that he was sitting out here alone when she'd just been given some good advice by one of his friends, so she decided to heed Carl's advice and push a little. "So, tell me about yours."

"My what?"

"Your family."

"There's not much to tell. They still live in Wilkerton, North Carolina, where Ashlee and Harrison and I grew up."

He sipped again and stretched his long legs out in front of him, as though that one line covered his entire family history.

"Do you have brothers and sisters?"

"Uh-huh." More silence.

"I could get more information out of Google."

"There's nothing to tell."

"No one in the world has nothing to tell about their family." Whether good, bad, loving or harsh, a family affected a person. There were always stories. Kendall thought of a few of her own, and one sprang immediately to mind. Her mother had tried for weeks to get her a Cabbage Patch doll the year they were all the rage; it was the single thing Kendall wanted for Christmas. Her mother had visited every store in the greater Portland area and finally, in desperation, called every relative and friend she knew. Finally an aunt had lined up in Kansas City when a new shipment of the dolls arrived. Somewhere, packed away in her mother's house, was that doll whom Kendall had called Sukie for reasons she could no longer even remember. It was a silly story, but it told a great deal about Kendall's family, she thought. How her mother wanted to make Christmas special, and how single-minded she could be when she set her sights on something. Like mother, like daughter.

But Dylan didn't reply. He didn't even glance her way, merely looked out over the enclave of trailers that housed the drivers and their families.

"How come I've never met your folks? They don't come to races."

"No. They don't."

She tried another tack. "They must be so proud of you, knowing you're a national celebrity."

"I guess."

More silence.

"This conversation is about as painful as pulling out my own toenails," she snapped.

"Then maybe we should change the subject," he suggested helpfully.

"Fine," she said, totally frustrated. "Don't tell me." She rose to her feet and headed inside.

"G'night," he called softly.

She was too well-brought-up and too mature to ignore him completely, but too miffed to offer a proper good-night. She made a noncommittal grunt.

Tomorrow another race. Another kiss. Then they'd pack up and move on again, to the next race, the next kiss.

She entered the trailer slowly, realizing that being a good-luck charm was, well, losing its charm for her. Now that she realized she was in love with Dylan, she could no longer accept the live-each-day-to-the-fullest fun and games of the past weeks.

It wasn't Dylan's fault. It was hers.

She loved him, and he was too much of a coward to let her into even the tiniest corner of his life. Except when he kissed her. It wasn't luck traveling between them then like sparks of lightning; it was magic.

For a moment she stood there, not flipping on a light, not doing anything but staring ahead into the darkened trailer. What was she doing?

Carl Edwards was right. Dylan was old enough to grow up and act like a man. He was old enough to stop playing games and settle down, and so was she. Strong and honest, she reminded herself.

She turned around and stalked back out again. Dylan was still sitting where she'd left him. He didn't hear her coming at first so she had a moment to study him, sitting there with a half-drunk soda clenched in his hand and the loneliest expression on his face. She wanted to comfort him but she was too mad.

"Dylan," she said, loud enough that he snapped his head her way.

"I thought you were turning in."

"I was. I need to talk to you."

He looked wary and she bet he wished he'd ducked into his own bed when he'd had the chance and pulled the covers over his head. "What about?"

"I need to make plans to head home. I've had a wonderful time, but I can't keep following you around from racetrack to racetrack. There's no need anymore. Ashlee and Harrison are gone and—"

"What about my luck?"

She smiled at him. "Your luck is going to be fine without me."

He rose to his feet. "Is this some punishment because I wouldn't blab all my childhood traumas to you? What are you? My therapist?"

"No. Of course not." Then she realized she wasn't being completely honest. "Well, maybe a little." She scuffed her foot against the ground, shifting a pebble. "I don't think it's enough for me to be your lucky charm. I thought we were friends, and then you won't let me into your life in the most basic way."

"I hurt your feelings," he said softly.

She nodded. "A little."

For a second there was silence between them. Somewhere out there, the partyers were at it, but here it was quiet. He rose to his feet and then pulled her against his chest, wrapping his arms around her. "I'm sorry," he murmured into her hair.

She leaned into him, loving the feel of him, the warm, muscular body, the smell of laundry soap and shampoo. The scent of his skin. He rubbed her back in a gesture that was comforting and that left her yearning for more. Somehow they'd become friends, but she didn't want to be his friend. She wanted his love.

"I don't think I can do this anymore," she said, not moving, enjoying being wrapped in his arms too much. She was weak, she knew that, but soon enough she'd be gone and it was so nice to be held by this special man.

"I didn't mean to shut you out." She felt his breath against her hair. "Your friendship means a lot to me."

Well, it wasn't a declaration of love, but friendship was something. At least he admitted she meant that much to him.

For a while they stayed there, his arms wrapped around her, his steady hand running up and down her spine. Then he spoke. "I've got a younger sister. She lives in town near my parents."

It wasn't much, but it was a start. He'd opened the door a crack. "Are you close?"

"No."

She didn't want to pry, but she didn't want to walk away, either. It was up to him now.

Finally he said, still talking into her hair so she

couldn't see his face, "They're a good family. We grew apart, that's all. My family isn't into racing. They pretty much stay close to home and I respect that. If I'm home, I visit. That's all there is to it."

And then Kendall the risk avoider took a very big risk. "Dylan," she said, "I want to meet your family."

She felt him go rigid, his muscles turning into steel armor. "Well, it's not going to happen." He pulled away then.

Push, Carl had said, and right now she was acting pushier than she ever had in her life. Her stomach felt wobbly as she made herself stand there and look at him with a steely glare she was copying from him. "That's my deal. If you want me to stay on as your good-luck charm until my leave is over, then I want to meet your family."

She expected him to say, "Pack your bags. I'll drive you to the airport." She expected at least that he'd blow up and tell her in a much louder fashion that his family was none of her business. But he didn't. He stuck his hands in his back pockets, took in a breath so deep she could see his chest expand with it.

"When?"

She couldn't believe she'd made him consider introducing her to his family. Her heart sang at the implication that she was more important to him than he'd let her believe. "This week. After the race."

"What misguided, do-gooding impulse is making you do this?"

Because we're friends, she thought, and friends help each other. "I want to see where you come from and meet your family."

"One dinner. One meal, that's it. That's my deal. Take it or leave it." He had his warrior's face on.

But his fierceness didn't scare her. She'd already won. "I'll take your deal."

"Okay, then. After tomorrow's race we'll head to Wilkerton."

"I'm looking forward to it."

"That's a mistake you won't make twice."

CHAPTER FOURTEEN

THE PLANE dropped them off at an airfield that Dylan told her was about an hour's drive away from his home. He seemed remote and a little tense, and her stomach started to tighten with sympathy nerves. The trouble with being pushy is that when you got what you wanted, you had to bear the responsibility.

They picked up a car that turned out to be his, as a short and cordial conversation with a big-bellied guy named Butch indicated.

He handed her the keys. "You drive."

She stood there, heat from the concrete parking area radiating up into her feet. "You're kidding me."

"No. You have a license, don't you?"

"You get paid millions of dollars to drive professionally. I get paid to crunch numbers."

He tossed the keys up in the air and caught them. "You're a terrible driver, aren't you?"

"Certainly not. I happen to be a very good driver."

"Prove it."

In front of Butch, who was watching the whole drama with interest, she didn't want to make a big deal out of it. She said, "Fine," and snatched the keys from Dylan, walked around to the driver's side and let herself in.

She adjusted the black leather seat. She adjusted the rearview mirror and the side mirrors. Actually, side *mirror,* since she only now noticed that there was one missing. "You're missing a side mirror on the passenger side."

"Huh, you're right."

She put on her seat belt, checked carefully and pulled out of the parking space. "It's dangerous to drive without both side mirrors. You should get it fixed."

He didn't give her a hard time. "Okay."

"Is making me drive your way of punishing me for forcing you to come home and introduce me to your family?" she asked. She'd become a lot more direct since she'd known him. Communication was much easier, she'd discovered.

"No." He sounded surprised. "Sometimes I get tired of driving."

"Oh." She glanced his way. "So, you're not going to criticize my every move and tell me I'm doing everything wrong?"

"Only if you turn out to be a terrible driver. That was a very nice three-point turn, by the way," he said so politely she had to laugh.

"I should have warned you," he said as they pulled out of the airfield's parking lot onto a two-lane highway, "that whenever I come home there are a few people I have to see."

"That's fine," she said, thinking that anyone who was important to Dylan was going to be important to her, too.

The area around Wilkerton didn't look exactly booming economically.

"We're going to visit Bessy Standish," he said as she followed his directions and pulled off the highway and down a bumpy asphalt drive with weeds growing through the cracks. "She's the wife of the guy who gave me my first ride. Ed passed on a couple of years ago. He was good to me. They both were."

The white house was on the shabby side, but it was neat, with ruffled curtains hanging in the windows. The front porch dipped a little with age, but it had the same faded charm as the woman who opened the door and let out a cry of delight before pulling Dylan in for a hug that he returned with enthusiasm.

Bessy Standish was tall and big-boned and probably somewhere in her late seventies, but she had the sharp eyes and upright gait of a younger woman.

She walked them to the back of the house past formal rooms that looked dusty and unused, to the kitchen where the smell of baking filled the air. "I'm making pies for the church charity bazaar," she announced.

A box of apples sat on the floor beside a big, planked kitchen table, and a blanket of pastry with a rolling pin beside it covered the kitchen counter.

The woman wiped her hands on her apron and went to a spotless white fridge with a bowed front that appeared to be from the fifties. She opened it, removed a jug of iced tea and poured three tumblers full, which she set on the big table.

"Hope you don't mind if I carry on while we talk."

"Can I help?" Kendall asked, thinking it was going to take all day to turn that box of apples into pie.

"You both can," Bessy said, pointing them to the sink to wash up.

It was surprisingly peaceful in the big kitchen peeling apples. Dylan, Mr. Big Shot Race Car Driver, took to the homely task as though he'd peeled apples for pie hundreds of times before. She was suddenly glad she'd forced him to come home, even for this kernel of knowledge about him.

"So, Kendall," the woman said, peeling twice as fast as either of her guests, "how'd you meet our local hero?"

"We met in Charlotte," she said, deciding to leave the details well shrouded in mystery.

"Crazy scene in Charlotte. You don't seem like Dy's usual type."

"Thank you," she said.

That earned her a guffaw of laughter. "I like this one. She's classy." She turned to Kendall. "Not like some of the pretty little things I've seen him with. All boob, no brain." She glanced down. "You've got enough boob, but you seem like you've got some brains to go with it."

Kendall shot a helpless look at Dylan, but he was giving her one of his glinting smiles—the kind where he seemed to be laughing at her without being too obvious about it. Then he dropped his gaze back to the apple he was peeling.

"Thank you," she said again.

"You finish school?"

She'd anticipated that his family might give her the third degree, but not that a former employer's wife would be similarly interested in her qualifications to be Dylan's partner on the road. She blinked. "I have my master's degree. In math."

The woman fanned herself. "Well, la-di-da." She

glanced up at Dylan. "Did you tell her your granddaddy ran in the first race in Daytona Beach?"

"It didn't come up." Among all the stories of his family she hadn't heard.

"I knew. I researched Dylan on the Internet."

"Hah! They put his granddaddy on the Internet?"

"Yes. They did."

"Well, I never. Wouldn't ol' Pete chuckle like a son of a gun if he knew that. Crazy that a bunch of guys racing on sand could start a million-dollar industry."

Billion-dollar, but neither of them bothered to correct her.

"If the South had won the war, it would be the national sport now, I reckon." She began slicing the peeled apples into a big, green ceramic bowl with astonishing speed. "So, Dylan, what brings you down here in the middle of the season?"

"I wanted Kendall to meet everybody," he said.

Not exactly the way it had happened, but an interpretation she liked very much. The words certainly earned the pair of them another glance, as sharp and swift as the knife Bessy was wielding. She didn't say anything, but once again Kendall was conscious of a nervous tightening in her belly. What wasn't being said seemed to echo loudly in the room.

"I like this one, Dy," the woman said.

"I like her, too. She brings me good luck."

Another hearty guffaw answered him. "I know, honey. I watch the races. You keep kissin' her like you do and them sportscasts are going to need an *R* rating."

"Really," Kendall said, feeling flustered. "It's only a silly routine that makes the fans happy."

In answer she received another sharp glance, but this one had a smile to go with it. "I'm not blind, child."

"You going to give us one of the pies for all this work?" Dylan asked some time later, when the fruit box was empty and Kendall had a cramp in her apple-peeling hand.

"You want a pie, you come to the bake sale. It'll cost you five dollars and the money will help fund the new preemie wing in the hospital."

"I already made a donation to that," Dylan said. He didn't say any more, but Kendall knew he gave significant sums to charity.

Bessy, however, remained unimpressed. "Every five dollars counts," she said.

After they'd finished pie-making and their tea and emerged into the heavy warmth of late afternoon, Kendall felt optimistic that bringing Dylan home was a good idea. Hoping to appear cool and unruffled when she met Dylan's parents, she turned on the air-conditioning when she restarted the car. Remembering the Caesar salad she'd eaten for lunch, she dug in her bag for breath mints.

"Would you like a mint?" she asked Dylan.

"Why? You planning on kissing me?"

"No. I don't want anchovy-and-garlic breath when I meet your family."

"You can brush your teeth at my place."

"You have a home in Wilkerton?"

She'd assumed he'd be staying with his family and she'd put up at a hotel. This was the first time he'd mentioned having his own place.

"Sure. I like my own space. We'll stay there."

This was a small town. "Will it cause trouble for you if I stay at your house?"

"Honey, it'll cause trouble for me if you don't. I have a reputation to keep up. Besides, I want Ashlee and Harrison hearing about how we're inseparable. Got it?"

He directed her to the next highway turnoff and soon she found herself driving through tree-lined streets bordered by small houses and gardens, neatly kept. They passed a small shopping plaza, two churches, a war memorial, a park and then a row of stately homes that sat on acreages. There was a body of water behind them that she thought was a broad, slow-moving river. "Oh, how lovely," she said.

"Ashlee's living in the fancy one with the yellow trim," he informed her. She wasn't surprised that Harrison Bryant would have one of the best houses in town.

The antebellum mansion suited Ashlee, too, she thought.

She wondered which one belonged to Dylan, who was most likely the richest man in town. But he didn't tell her to stop, so she kept driving. Past the mansions, past the not-quite mansions, past the minimansions that were all house and no land, past a school, another park. Then they came to a T intersection.

"Turn right," he told her.

She discovered she'd guessed correctly that the body of water she'd glimpsed was a wide, lazy-moving river when they crossed over it on a wooden bridge.

It felt as though the river separated city from country, for as soon as they'd crossed, she noticed the now-familiar fields of tobacco and animals grazing in the distance.

Dylan's place was about a fifteen-minute drive

outside Wilkerton. At his direction, she turned down a tree-shaded gravel lane and bumped her way down to a modern home. It was styled like a farmhouse, but she could tell it was new. There were fields of crops, a few horses grazing on a back paddock and then the dark green of trees.

"How much land do you have?" she asked.

"'Bout fifty acres."

"And you farm it?"

"Sure. Well, obviously I hire a guy to farm it for me, but someday I can see myself setting up as a farmer."

The lifestyle seemed so slow and tranquil she couldn't imagine Dylan settling. But she supposed he was well able to afford as many visions of himself as he wanted. Besides, the farm must provide a bit of economic benefit to the area, even if only in creating jobs for a farmer and some hired hands.

It was clear the farmhouse had been updated when Dylan directed her to drive around the side and into a freestanding, three-car garage.

Once she entered the house, she was amazed at how it seemed like a real home. It had more character than the house he kept outside Charlotte. That was it, she realized. That was a house he owned. This was his home. She followed him into a kitchen that was bright and cheery. Pine cabinets, granite counters, steel appliances—and there were plenty of them, including an espresso machine that would have looked at home in Starbucks.

The main living area was done in a great-room style so there was no division, merely a counter bar that separated the kitchen from the eating area. The big, oval oak table and chairs emitted the scent of lemon oil, and there was a vase of fresh tulips in the middle. Clearly, Dylan had housekeeping help. Live-in?

His living room furniture was mostly leather and she was pleased to see she hadn't been completely wrong. Over a river-rock fireplace mantel hung a plasma TV.

There was also art on the walls. Modern pieces and a couple of metal sculptures.

"The bedrooms are this way," Dylan said, leading the way down a hallway. They passed several doors as he led her to the last one.

The guest room at the end of the hall was decorated in soft blues with cream accents. It was a soothing, pretty room with an en suite bathroom.

"Make yourself at home," he said. "I'm going to take a look around my land." She didn't miss the tiny inflection of pride when he mentioned "my land."

She unpacked and headed to the window of her bedroom and stared out at some of the prettiest countryside she'd ever seen. There was something restful about this place, and the house seemed to exude—what? She closed her eyes for a second and decided it was peace.

Once more, she felt this odd sense of Dylan having a side to him she'd glimpsed once or twice but never truly believed. There was the crazy, restless, hard-driven, fast-driving NASCAR hero and then there was the quiet, contemplative man. It seemed this was where that other man lived.

She walked through the quiet house, peeking into all the doors down the hall on her way back to the great room. There were four bedrooms in all. Dylan's bedroom had a soaring ceiling, an enormous bed and a bathroom that reminded her of an upscale spa. The other bedrooms were set up as guest rooms with a simple white duvet and pine furniture. Each, she noted, had its own bathroom. It made her think the rooms were designed more with guests in mind than family.

There was also a fully equipped office with a couple of top-of-the-line computers, a wall of filing cabinets, a bar fridge and a round conference table in one corner. There were a couple of racing posters on the wall. Interesting. It was the only room in the house that held any hint of its owner's profession.

When she returned to the great room, she heard the dull roar of an engine and glanced outside to see a yellow tractor rolling by, with a familiar-looking driver in a navy ball cap.

In his absence, she checked out the kitchen. The cupboards were stocked, the fridge contained fresh milk, cheese and eggs, yogurt and fruit—which must be for her benefit—and some cold cuts and beer for Dylan's. There was also wine and juice, meat in the freezer section and bread in the bread bin. They weren't going to starve out here, and she wasn't going to have to run to the grocery store in town.

Within an hour, she'd unpacked, ironed a few things, showered off the grime of the day and changed into khaki shorts and a bright teal cotton sleeveless shirt.

Then she walked out to the kitchen and paused there. She had no idea what his plans were, and this was his turf. A low, rumbling sound like a roadway construction crew came to her ears. She strode to the big picture window and looked out to find the yellow tractor zooming by again. If a tractor could speed, this one was going to break records. She shook her head. The man was a nutcase and she couldn't stand around here waiting for his lordship to gallop by on his tractor and remember she was here.

Shoving on one of the caps she found on pegs by the kitchen door, she let herself out and hiked off in the direction of the speeding tractor. The sun felt warm on her skin, the earth springy and fertile, and she'd take it any day over the speedways, though wherever Dylan went it seemed the sound of engines went with him. The tractor rumbled along, grumbling at the unnecessary speed, and getting louder as she approached. Dylan didn't seem to be doing anything more useful than riding around, but then she caught sight of him and realized he was surveying his land. There was a look of pride on his face and a sort of awe, as though he couldn't believe this was his.

Maybe that was it, she thought. He was comparing this place to the speedways, too. This was everything the racing series wasn't. Quiet, bucolic, slow of pace, with horses outnumbering motorized vehicles. As she walked over a grassy hill, she saw a large pond sparkling in the sunshine and a hawk swooped over it, trailing its shadow across the water's surface.

She felt an urge to run down the other side of the hill, and, because there was nobody but a crazy race car driver to see her do it, she let herself go. She laughed aloud as her feet pounded down the grass, almost but not quite losing control. When she slowed she found Dylan was watching her, a big grin on his face. She knew his expression mirrored her own.

He gestured for her to join him. She hiked back up

the grassy hill and when she came abreast of the tractor he held out a hand and she jumped up beside him.

She'd never ridden any kind of farm equipment before and was surprised at how comfy it was. The seat was leather and she felt high off the ground as she surveyed the land through the dusty window.

"What do you think?"

"It's absolutely beautiful," she said.

"I like it."

"I know."

"You here for the official tour?"

"No. I'm here to ask if you want me to cook dinner tonight?"

Some of the light went out of his face. "No. We'll eat with my folks. They're expecting us."

She forced a smile, refusing to let his unhappiness at the dinner plan mar her mood. "Okay. Is there anything special I should wear for dinner?"

"You look great like you are. I'll put this thing away and we'll head out. You'll see the house where I grew up."

"I can't wait."

He laughed, a short, bitter sound. "Later, I'll remind you that you said that."

CHAPTER FIFTEEN

SHE DECIDED to change. She needed a meet-the-parents outfit. She chose a demure white cotton dress that left her arms bare, summer sandals and low-key jewelry. Kendall followed the paint-by-numbers face for day wear and toned it down a little more.

When she emerged from her room, she found Dylan in the living area pacing. She was glad she had changed. He wore a pale gray suit with a conservative silk tie, white shirt and polished black loafers. His hair was neatly brushed and he was freshly shaven. She'd become so used to him dressing in casual clothes and his racing uniform that she was momentarily startled by the transformation. The man looked gorgeous, though the suit didn't really tame the wildness she'd seen in him from the beginning. If anything, his tame outerwear only made her more aware of the wildness he carried with him everywhere. His scar seemed more visible than usual, the planes of his face more rugged.

When he caught her staring at him, he said, "What?" He put a hand to his chest. "Is my tie crooked?"

She blinked at him in surprise. "You're nervous."

"Don't be crazy."

But the impression wouldn't leave her. "I've watched

you race a car at one hundred and eighty miles an hour, seen you handle media scrums and get mobbed by fans, and you were as cool as a cucumber. Now, you go for dinner at your parents' house and you're nervous."

"I'm irritable at the big waste of time, that's all. But, you wanted to meet the folks, so you'll meet the folks."

"Do you want me to drive?"

"No. You drive like a girl." This from the guy who'd promised he wouldn't criticize her driving.

"That's funny. Usually, I drive like a sixteen-year-old boy who just got his license," she said sweetly, wishing he'd calm down since she was picking up on his discomfort and beginning to share it. What was wrong with these people who had given birth to him?

As she sat beside him in the car, she wondered why she'd made such a big deal about meeting the family. This wasn't her business, it wasn't her world. Dylan and she as a couple were an accident of fate. He liked her. Sometimes he was amused by her, happy that a few kisses were keeping the fans enthralled and Ashlee at bay. None of that gave her any right to barge into his personal life or intrude on his family. Yet on some level, she knew she had to do this, if not for them, then for him.

So she squelched the nerves dancing in her stomach and looked forward to meeting the people who had helped make Dylan the man he was.

The house was a huge mansion. When they drove up the circular drive shadowed by ancient oaks she whispered, "You grew up here?"

"Yep." He didn't sound thrilled about it. She wasn't sure what she'd expected. A trailer park? No. If she'd pictured Dylan's home at all, she'd imagined a middle-class home in a decent area, something like what she'd had as a child.

He pulled the car to a halt and to her immense surprise hooked her with an arm and kissed her. This wasn't the racetrack and she wasn't prepared. She was so surprised she forgot to be careful, so that when his lips touched hers, she sighed and melted against him. He raised his head, studied her face and said, "I need some luck before I go in there."

He didn't release her and she didn't move, so they sat staring at each other. She heard her own heart beating, felt his breath on her face. His eyes were serious, and in that moment she felt something shift. Some awareness she hadn't felt before. She could barely breathe.

"You're so sweet," he said softly. Then kissed her again, deeper, longer, and she tasted sadness, frustration, pain. She wanted to comfort him, tell him everything would be okay. It was a stupid idea, this dinner, drive on.

He pulled away slowly and the spell broke. She jerked in a breath.

"Don't let them intimidate you," he warned, and then got out of the car while she dug frantically into her purse for her new lip gloss and touched up her lips so she was as close to perfect-looking as she could be when Dylan helped her out of the car.

A uniformed servant greeted them at the door to the mansion, opening it almost as soon as Dylan had knocked.

She entered a hushed hall furnished with antiques that fit so perfectly she wondered if they'd been pur-chased new when the house was built a century and a half ago. A gorgeous, huge flower arrangement on a highly polished drum table reminded her of those in five-star hotel lobbies. There was a scent of lemon furniture polish in the air.

The maid led them to an imposing reception room, she supposed you'd call it, where a couple sat on gold furniture drinking something out of heavy crystal glasses.

"Good evening, Dylan," said a gaunt woman in a navy Chanel suit, navy pumps and a string of fat pearls. Her blond hair gleamed with highlights from platinum to deep gold. Her eyes were cold and blue, and her face so unlined and serene that she could advertise Botox. Good evening, Dylan? The woman was his mother and hadn't seen him in months, yet she greeted him like a remote and formal acquaintance.

The man in the room was the perfect bookend to his wife. Imposing, silver-haired and large, he looked prosperous, snobby and well-pleased with himself. From him, Dylan had inherited the hazel eyes and the chin. "Son," he said with a nod.

Dylan placed a hand on her lower back, possibly to stop her from bolting. "Mother, Father, I'd like you to meet Kendall Clarke."

"Good evening, Miss Clarke," said his mother with a tiny movement of her lips.

"Good evening. Thank you for inviting me."

Something about the way Dylan's mother looked her over reminded her that her dress wasn't particularly expensive and that no designer would admit to having a hand in its creation.

She felt dowdy and out of place in the house that reminded her more of a museum than a family home.

When invited to sit, she perched at the edge of a chair whose upholstery seemed too expensive to sit on. How did anyone relax in a place like this? Then she glanced around and realized no one in the room was relaxed, least of all Dylan, who sat in a gilded chair she thought might be Louis XV and wore the expression she recognized as the same one he assumed when a fan got too personal. It was his remote, don't-take-one-step-closer expression and she liked him least when he wore it.

Her arms felt chilled and she knew gooseflesh was rising in a most unattractive manner. The Hargreaves had obviously cranked up the AC.

As if the atmosphere wasn't chilly enough.

"Your sister will be a little late," Mrs. Hargreave informed them with another of those tiny lip movements that constituted a smile. Kendall was aware of an insane impulse to tell raucous jokes simply to see what would happen to her face if she ever laughed. "Mary Beth, Dylan's sister, is an attorney."

A pause ensued. "Are you an attorney also, sir?" she asked Mr. Hargreave.

His wife answered, her nostrils flaring slightly as though her dry sherry might be the wrong vintage. "Dylan's father is a judge. The men of his family have served as judges for over a century."

"Until I came along," Dylan said, speaking for the first time since he'd introduced her. "I am the black sheep of the family. The skeleton in the Hargreave closet."

No one corrected him. This man who received so much adulation she didn't think it was good for his ego was admitting to being a disappointment to his family, and his family wasn't saying a word. She couldn't stand it.

"You're not the first skeleton though, are you? I believe I heard that your grandfather took part in the very first race at Daytona."

Dylan shot her a glance that had some of his usual devilry in it. But if she'd managed to make him feel better for a minute, she'd done herself no favors with his parents.

"That is a part of our family history we prefer not to discuss," Dylan's dad said. For a second she wondered if this whole setup was some bizarre practical joke, as if Dylan had hired the town's museum and a couple of actors to play his parents. Who wouldn't love to have a stock car pioneer in their past? Or a NASCAR hero for a son? This was the most ridiculous evening she'd ever spent five minutes in. And yet something about Dylan's face told her this wasn't a joke. He'd actually grown up with these cold snobs.

Wow.

"Would you like a cocktail?" Mr. Hargreave asked.

"Thank you. White wine?"

"Dylan? Scotch?"

"Sure."

She blinked. She'd never seen him drink anything but his sponsor's beer and little enough of that.

While Mr. Hargreave poured drinks, his wife filled them in on local goings-on. It was a neutral subject, and so she let herself relax. But not for long.

"As you know, Dylan, I'm on the board of directors of the hospital foundation. We're raising funds for a new preemie wing."

Dylan made a sound of assent. Kendall waited for his mother to thank him for his donation, or perhaps ask him for one so that he could tell her he'd already contributed, but what she said was, "Ashlee serves on the committee, as well."

Kendall received her glass of wine and took a deep swallow.

There was silence in the room.

"Don't you want to know how your wife is?"

"Ex-wife, Mom, and I know how she is. She's fine. Kendall and I were at her wedding."

His mother shifted her pearls a quarter of an inch to the left. "You two made a lovely couple."

"Yeah, well, she and Harrison make a lovely couple, too."

"They're in town, so I invited them for dinner tonight—"

"I wish you wouldn't do that, Mom."

"Nonsense. We're old family friends. In any case, they weren't able to make it. But she sends her regards." She sighed, her hair glinting like the gilt on the Louis XV furniture. "I miss having Ashlee in the family."

"She hated racing, Mother. She hated my whole lifestyle."

"Of course she did. You were destined for the law. Everyone knew it, including Ashlee."

"Everyone knew it but me," Dylan said.

"If you had any idea how much you've let everyone down—"

"Have you ever seen Dylan race?" Kendall interrupted. She couldn't stand this. Dylan could muscle his way past the fastest, the meanest and the sneakiest of NASCAR, but here he was getting pulverized by his mother.

"I think I hear Mary Beth arriving," Mr. Hargreave said.

They all turned to the door as though to an empty stage, waiting for the star to appear.

Mary Beth Hargreave didn't disappoint. She walked in exactly as a diva should, with a model's walk, a business tycoon's power suit and a feminine version of Dylan's face. She had her mother's slim build and a pair of heels that smote Kendall with envy.

The evening went down another notch.

"Move over, bro," she said, walking toward Dylan and sitting beside him. "The favorite child has returned."

Kendall blinked, then looked at Dylan, ready to haul him out of there, but he looked happier than he had all evening. His sister kissed him on the cheek.

"Mary Beth, dear. Not in front of guests."

But Mary Beth pretty much ignored her mother and came toward Kendall with her hand outstretched. "Hi, I'm Mary Beth."

"Kendall Clarke."

Sharp hazel eyes surveyed her. "Hey, Dy, is this one an exotic dancer, too?"

"Mary Beth, please."

Too stunned to speak, she glanced over at Dylan to find his mouth had kicked up on one side. At least somebody was finding pleasure in this hideous situation.

He didn't answer and, after almost squeezing the feeling out of her fingers, Mary Beth let her hand go. "The last woman Dylan brought home for dinner was a stripper."

"No, I'm—"

"She wasn't a stripper," Dylan said. "She was a teacher."

"She taught pole dancing."

"Really?" Kendall was amazed that he'd dare bring any woman home who wasn't a gentle Southern belle.

"Yep. Before that he brought home a country singer we'd never heard of and will never hear of. She chewed gum nonstop and called us all sugar." Mary Beth sank down gracefully. "She had very nice hair, though. Big, you know?"

"Would you like a cocktail, dear?"

"Thanks, Dad. I'll have a Scotch." She eased back. "Let's see, was the short-order cook the one before the country singer? Or was it that waitress whose big claim to fame was that she was Miss April in the mid-nineties?"

"Dylan never goes out with any respectable women," his mother agreed, not seeming to speak to anyone in particular. "Not since Ashlee. If only you'd—"

Kendall had been around Dylan—and, even better, the NASCAR wives and girlfriends, who could be as gossipy as any other bunch of women—long enough to know that he didn't date women like that. Interesting. He only brought big-haired, gum-chewing, nude-posing, pole-dancing women home to his family.

But his family didn't appreciate or understand him. They'd wanted a judge and they'd ended up with a race car driver. Instead of being proud of Dylan's accomplishments, they looked down on him. Of course, Dylan being Dylan, he would play up to the image they had of him as a wild man.

For the first time since she'd entered this house, she smiled. He was an emotional teenager acting out. A lot of things started to make sense. She was so glad she'd made him bring her here.

"So, I've seen you on TV kissing my brother. Is that your full-time job?" the power-suited sister asked.

Dylan's mouth settled back to its straight line again. What? Did he think she didn't understand him? Did he believe she was going to disappoint him? Oh, no. Not tonight.

"I'm between jobs," she said.

"Unemployed," Dylan's dad said to his mom in a tone that suggested they didn't want to know what kind of jobs she was between.

Mary Beth was obviously not a sweep-unpleasant-ness-under-the-rug type. She moved to sit beside Kendall, looking interested, and Kendall revised her first impression. She had a feeling that, in spite of the fact she'd entered the family firm, as it were, Mary Beth was more like Dylan than she was like his uptight parents.

"What kind of work do you do?"

However, as much as she thought she might like Mary Beth under normal circumstances, these weren't normal, at least not for her. Having brought Dylan here under protest to a home where he clearly wasn't appreciated, she needed him to know she was on his side.

"I'm in the service industry," she said.

"Probably a waitress," Dylan's mother said with disdain.

"Which month did you pose?" Mary Beth asked.

She shot a glance at her date, who had settled back in his chair and was watching her. "Actually, I'm an actress," she said, remembering how she'd first met Dylan.

He sent her a wink, and she felt as though he'd kissed her.

"Let's move into the dining room, shall we?" Mrs. Hargreave rose and led the way, ending further discussion of her occupation.

Dinner was, if possible, more strained than the cocktail hour. The dining room was frighteningly perfect. A rectangular table set with fancy china, pressed linens and crystal was laid for five. A silver bowl of roses sat in the middle of a tablecloth that had been ironed so there wasn't a crease, a line, not the tiniest wrinkle. The cloth lay heavily on the table, cascading off in perfect folds as though it had been painted on. The roses were cream-colored, each one coming into bloom as though the bush had been ordered to produce an entire dining table's crop of roses that very afternoon.

Mrs. Hargreave took her place at the head of the table and invited her son to sit on her right. The two women were directed to sit on either side of his father who sat, very correctly, at the other end of the table from his wife. Kendall was mildly surprised that there wasn't a sixth diner simply to provide perfect symmetry to the table setting. Perhaps the idea of subjecting one of their friends to Dylan's questionable date made an uneven table preferable to social ridicule.

She ended up being the one with the empty place yawning between her and Dylan's mother, so she felt like the odd one out.

A uniformed maid appeared, followed by a second,

so they were all served their dinner at once. Dylan's father turned to Mary Beth. "What's your opinion on the Lund case?" he asked her.

The two were soon buried in a complex conversation that no one outside the law profession could possibly follow. Dylan's father talked to his sister with animation and pleasure. He'd never addressed one direct remark to Dylan except to ask if he wanted another drink.

Stress crawled up her legs like fire ants.

She glanced over at Dylan to find him staring at his plate while his mother leaned forward, looking past him and listening with full attention to her daughter.

How could she have been so wrong? She'd imagined Dylan as the favored child, something she'd seen on more than one occasion, where the daughter was overshadowed by a brother. The male heir. At least the favoritism in this house had a feminist slant. Except that Mary Beth had followed in her father's footsteps, in some ways becoming the son Dylan would never be.

Kendall wanted to hate Mary Beth on principle, with her power suit and her legal mind, the way she'd usurped Dylan's place in the family order. Yet somehow, she couldn't do it. There was just enough of Dylan in his sister for Kendall to withhold judgment. More, there was an expression on her face that suggested she knew their family dynamic was whacked but what was she supposed to do about it?

No, Kendall thought, she'd at least wait until dessert before banishing Mary Beth to the mental disaster zone where she'd consigned his parents within minutes of meeting them.

It wasn't the longest dinner she'd ever sat through. She had, after all, attended her fair share of actuarial dinners that made up for in longevity what they lacked in wit. But this was right up there with the most unpleasant meals of her life. Perfect food and wines to complement each course couldn't cover up the tension between Dylan and his family.

A couple of times, she tried to bring him into the conversation. That earned her glares from him, blank looks from his mother and father and a look of interest from the sister.

After dinner, when she hoped they might make their escape, Dylan's mother suddenly turned to Kendall and said, "You seem very interested in Dylan's career. Perhaps you'd like to see his collection of school trophies."

"Mother," Dylan said in a warning tone.

"I'd love to see his trophies," she said. Finally, some sense that they took pride in their son.

Dutifully, she followed his mother into the library, a grand old room smelling of fine leather and dust. Books lined the walls, and the room contained several seating areas and a huge, old desk with a top-of-the-line computer sitting incongruously on it. Dylan's mother led Kendall to a glass case that contained trophies, cups and ribbons.

"Here is Dylan's trophy from the debating team in high school. They went all the way to the national championships. They came second."

"The debating team. Very impressive." She glanced up to see the entire family had followed.

"And here's the medal for winning the highest score

in math." She sighed. "He was such a bright boy, with such a promising future."

Not one single bit of racing paraphernalia was contained in that cabinet of pride. It was as though Dylan had ceased to exist when he quit the debating team and stopped acing math.

"You know," Kendall said brightly, "you should clear a space in that cabinet for when Dy wins the NASCAR NEXTEL Cup."

The cabinet shut with a decided click.

For an uncomfortable moment, no one said anything or even moved.

Kendall broke the silence.

"Thank you for a lovely evening, but we should get going. I have an audition tomorrow." She smiled at them all, doing her best to look like a bimbo. "I need to go home and run through my line."

CHAPTER SIXTEEN

SHE AND DYLAN emerged from the house, and she felt a breath of relief flow out of her body.

"Wow, that was—"

The sound of the door opening and closing behind them stopped her.

"Hey, wait," his sister called out.

They turned and waited.

"How long are you in town for?" she asked Dylan.

He shrugged. "Not long. A week, maybe."

"Don't be a stranger."

"I should hate you."

"But you don't. You can't help yourself." She turned to Kendall. "It was nice to meet you, Kendall. I hope I get to see you again."

"Thanks. I—" She stopped to think. "Amazingly, I enjoyed meeting you, too."

Mary Beth took out her business card and handed it to Kendall. "Call me. We'll do lunch. If you want all the dirt on my bro, I am your woman."

"We're probably going to be really busy," Dylan said, moving toward the car.

"What kind of dirt are we talking?" Kendall wanted to know. "Embarrassing moments on the sports field?"

"The entire blooper reel of his life will be laid out before you."

There was a flurry of metallic clicks as Dylan hit the automatic key pad.

"Old girlfriends?"

"I know all."

"Kendall?" Dylan said with a warning note.

"Coming. Would tomorrow be too soon?"

Mary Beth grinned at her. "I'll clear my schedule."

"You're not having lunch with my sister," Dylan ordered when she got into the car.

"I have a date. I never break my promise." She turned to him, his profile was uncompromising. He lifted a hand and jerked his tie loose. "What are you afraid she'll tell me?"

"Nothing. She'll tell you nothing. She's a trouble-maker, that's all."

"Not the only one in the family, Mr. I-only-date-scary-women-with-big-hair-who-pose-nude-for-men's-magazines."

The hard lines around his jaw softened. "I can't help myself. They bring out the worst in me."

WHEN THEY arrived home, she said, "Dylan?"

"Yeah."

"I'm sorry. I had no right to push myself into your family like that."

"It's okay."

He pulled off his jacket and tie and tossed them over the back of the couch.

"Are we really staying a week?"

"We might as well, now we're here. There's a break

in the racing schedule, I've got some jobs to do around here and I can sure use a rest."

"And I can finally start getting my résumé organized."

"Don't," he said with a sudden scowl.

"You know, you've been really good for me. I had so little faith in myself when I jumped into your car. Now, I'm seriously considering not going back to my company. The opening's been delayed and I don't think they're in any big rush to have me back. Maybe it's time for me to move on. There are other jobs, other firms."

"Don't," he repeated.

"Why?" she asked softly.

He moved forward until he stood directly in front of her. He pulled her into his arms. "Because I ain't nearly done with you yet."

"Well, that's good. Because I'm not nearly done with you, either."

The sad truth was she was fairly certain he'd be done with her a lot sooner than she would be done with him. Like maybe ever. Well, she'd worry about that—and about an ensuing broken heart—when the time came. Until then, she planned to enjoy every minute. Even the kind of sad minutes, like this one. There was so much she wanted to say to him, about the evening and the strange dynamics of his family, but she didn't know where to begin or if he'd welcome her curiosity, so she said nothing.

He stroked her back in long, soothing movements, but she felt he was looking for comfort as much as he was giving it. He stroked her the way a hurting child might stroke a favorite stuffed animal or a beloved pet.

She squirmed a little at her own mental image of herself as the family mutt.

"Cold?" He rubbed a little faster.

"No. Not really." She decided to share a little of the truth with him. "I was thinking I'll be sorry when this is over."

"Then stay."

"I don't belong here. One day very soon, I'm going to have to go back to my own life, and the longer I stay, the harder it's going to be." She took a breath to steady herself, trying to make him understand without giving too much away—like the fact that she was very much afraid she was in love with him. "I'm not part of your world."

"Sure you are. I can't imagine what these last weeks would have been like without you."

"Probably they would have been very much like all the other weeks you raced when I wasn't around."

"The same, only with a lot less winning and a lot more losing. I know you think it's crazy and superstitious of us, but we've all seen the difference. You bring me and my team luck."

"That's nice, but statistically impossible, of course. A number of factors go into winning. Better—"

"Forget the luck, or the statistics. Nobody could have helped me out of the jam with Ashlee the way you did."

"That's another thing. I'm not a real girlfriend, either. I feel like I'm living somebody else's life. I keep pretending to be all these things I'm not. Even my clothes aren't my own."

"Now, honey, you can't tell me you like all those dirt- and mold-colored clothes better than the ones you're wearing now, because if you did I'd have to go against my principles and call a woman a liar."

She chuckled, as she knew he'd meant her to, but she wouldn't be fobbed off. "No. Of course I love these clothes. And I enjoy being part of your team. I'm having a wonderful time." Too wonderful. Much, much too wonderful.

"So everything's fine."

"No. Everything is not fine. I feel like I'm on leave from my own place in the world. I'm a planner, a... I look at the future and calculate things like life expectancy and risks associated with certain lifestyles, and I have to tell you that what I'm doing is extremely high-risk for me."

"Why?" The single word was said simply, but she thought he sounded hurt.

She tipped her head back and tried to explain. "Because Cinderella doesn't always get the handsome prince. Sometimes the prince isn't for her, and she ends up back in her dead-end job. Don't you think that the longer she plays at being the princess, the harder it's going to be to go back?"

"This is total garbage. First off, you work in an insurance company. You don't sweep ashes. Second, I am no prince, and I have never for one second treated you like a princess."

She sighed softly. "No. But you made me feel like one."

"So, what are you saying? Are you looking for some kind of commitment? Because you know I never—"

"Of course you never," she interrupted him quickly. "I never expected anything or asked for it."

"Then what's the problem?"

"The problem is that now I want it." She heard her voice waver and cleared her throat, determined to be strong. She reached out for him and clasped his hand. "It's not your fault, Dylan. It's mine. I'm such an idiot. I never should have jumped into your car that day. I was hurt and angry and lost and I thought, for once I'm going to do something crazy, impulsive, wild. So I took a flying leap into a getaway car." She laughed softly, thinking about how ridiculous she must have looked to that line of actuaries watching in amazement.

"And you've had fun. We've had fun."

"Oh, yes, we have. More fun than I ever imagined. But Dylan…" She sucked in a breath and told him the truth, even though she knew it would ruin everything. "I've fallen in love with you."

THAT WAS strong and honest. Just the kind of statement Carl Edwards had said he was looking for from a woman. Unfortunately, Dylan didn't have that sort of reaction. Maybe he was looking for something else, she thought.

He didn't say anything, or move. She felt a tiny twitch in the hand that still clasped hers.

For a while she heard nothing but the soft sounds of their breathing and the crazy pounding of her heart.

"You know, Kendall," he said at last, "sometimes people get into situations and think they feel more than they do."

"No!" she shouted, amazed at the fury that possessed her. "No. Don't you dare throw it back at me. I feel what I feel and it's honest. I love you. I don't want anything from you. I know you don't love me back."

She swallowed, determined to hang on to control, or at least, if that wasn't possible, to stop herself from sobbing all over him. "I never expected that you would, but now I've so stupidly fallen in love with you, I don't think I can go on like this indefinitely."

"Maybe if you stick around, it will burn itself out. I'm no prize, you know."

She smiled. "I know. It's funny. At one time I thought I'd marry Marvin. We have so much in common. But I know now that I never loved him at all. At least I've learned to recognize my own feelings. I'll be okay, you know. I'm strong. But you have to make it easy for me to go."

"When?"

"I think I should go soon."

He looked at her, a slight frown pulling his brows together. "I'd like you to give me two weeks' notice."

"Two weeks' notice? Dylan, I kiss you before races. It's an unpaid, voluntary position. You want me to give you notice? Like a real job?"

"Yes."

She was about to tell him where he could put his notice when she stopped herself. Two weeks. Fourteen days. Half a month, give or take, before her dream would end. If she was smart, she'd go right away, but she wasn't that smart, or that strong. She had half a month to get both smarter and stronger. "Okay."

She didn't know what to do and she could tell he didn't, either. Normally there would be meetings or events to get ready for, but for the next few days there was nothing. So they stood there, slightly awkward. "Do you want anything?"

Apart from you to love me back? "No. I'm pretty tired. I think I'll turn in."

"Okay." He headed to the fridge, opened it, pulled out a beer and then put it back. He closed the fridge door and turned back to her. "I wish it could be different."

She nodded.

"Can we still stay here for the week? I want to show you around and maybe teach you to ride a horse."

She stared at him, at that rugged, too-handsome-for-his-own-good, and somehow sad, face. "I'd like that."

She walked over to stand in front of him and he looked down at her for a moment, serious eyes in a serious face. Then he lifted his hands to her hair and finally he kissed her.

Their kiss was soft and slow and tender, unlike it had ever been before. Was it because she'd admitted her feelings to him? Or because he'd spent a lousy evening with his family and he needed her comfort? She didn't know, but when he kissed her she saw the confusion in his gaze and the sadness. "I wish I could give you what you want," he said.

She raised her head up to touch her lips to his. "I'll never forget any of this." And because she was already so much braver than she'd ever believed possible, she said, "I love you."

He kissed her again and then clasped her fingers and held their joined hands against her heart.

Maybe he didn't love her back, but at that moment she'd never felt closer to another human being. Of course it wasn't going to last, but she wanted to know everything there was to know about this man, wanted to take memories with her that would live inside her, moments like this that she could bring out like photographs in an album, to pore over and savor.

"What do you want, Dylan?"

After a long moment, she heard him say, "I want to win the Cup."

"Statistically, that could still happen this year."

"Yes, my little actuary. Statistically, it could."

"And that's your life's ambition? To drive fast?" She didn't mean to sound unimpressed, but really. "You've already won two Cups. You've been clocked going faster than any driver ever."

"For one lap."

"But how many times can you break your own records? How many times can you keep winning?"

"A lot of times and not get bored."

And suddenly, it hit her with a powerful and instant insight. "That's it, isn't it? I think that's why you were in that nonwinning streak. You were bored. I made your life more interesting. I challenged you."

"You think I'm winning now because of you?"

It was the most egotistical, unscientific reckoning she'd ever made in her life. She didn't hesitate. "Yes, I do."

"So now you believe me about the luck?"

"No. I think I cured your boredom, at least temporarily." She tipped back her head to look him straight in the eye. "And I think you should figure out why that might be."

Kendall looked at him for a long time. She opened her mouth, then shook her head a little and closed her lips.

"What?" he asked.

She kissed him swiftly and headed off to her room.

CHAPTER SEVENTEEN

DYLAN WOKE with a leaden feeling in his gut. In the half-waking stage, he was conscious of something bad hanging over him and it took him a minute to figure out what it was.

Then it hit him. Kendall.

He was losing Kendall.

Why did she have to tell him she loved him? Then she'd gone straight to her room and shut the door leaving him feeling frustrated, foolish and somehow lonely. He'd been so tempted to follow her, to beg her to stay, to beg her to make this relationship of theirs more serious than a few kisses. She loved him, after all.

Maybe, if she was really his girlfriend, he could talk her into staying. She didn't want to go back to that company that didn't stand by her or appreciate her, and he hated to let her humiliate herself like that. Here, she was needed, respected, valued by the whole team and by a big chunk of the fans.

Dylan had everything to offer her but his love in return. Somehow he already knew that it wasn't enough. Kendall was a romantic, an all-or-nothing woman, and what he had to offer was pretty much nothing. It had been clear to him last night during that excruciating dinner with his parents that there was something genetically wrong with the Hargreaves. They were cold, unable to connect on that soul-deep level that Kendall obviously believed in.

He rolled out of bed and stomped into the shower, knowing that her best bet for finding a soul-deep love was to look far away from him.

He wasn't sure how she'd be this morning after the things they'd said to each other last night, but to his relief she seemed very much as she usually did first thing in the morning. Cheerful, energetic and all pulled together. She was sitting at the kitchen table with a mug of coffee in front of her, reading a magazine.

"'Morning," he said.

She rose and went to pour him coffee. "Good morning." She wore cream-colored jeans, a sleeveless green T-shirt with a scoop neck and a stylish belt. Her hair was still damp from her shower, and she smelled like lavender. He noticed that her skin had an extra glow and wondered if she'd forgotten her sunscreen yesterday.

He sat across from her at the table, pleased to find the atmosphere wasn't as tense as he'd feared. In fact, their talk and her declaration that she loved him might never have happened.

"I'm hoping you'll show me your land today."

"Sure."

"But first I'll make you breakfast."

"You don't have to cook for me, Kendall."

She gave him her sweet smile. "I know. But I have to do something to stay busy. Besides, I like to cook."

Since their conversation of last night was still fresh in his mind, he didn't call her on it, merely said, "I like my eggs cooked in bacon fat and runny."

"How do your arteries feel about that?"

"Kendall, you serve me any of that fresh fruit and organic granola crap and I swear you'll be sorry."

She glanced at him and he could have sworn she blushed.

"Hah," he said, watching her closely. "You were planning to, weren't you?"

"I'm not saying I was, and I'm not saying I wasn't. But olive oil is a lot healthier than bacon fat."

"If I want to taste olives, I'll eat olives."

"You are hopeless," she said, opening drawers. "I don't suppose you have an apron?"

"Oh, yeah. I use an apron all the time. Pink, frilly thing."

She muttered some more and then dug out a couple of checked cloths for drying dishes and wrapped one around her waist.

She rattled pots and pulled stuff out of the fridge and he poured more coffee. He was trying to decide whether to head outside and get the tractor out or sit in here and watch her work when the phone rang.

He scowled at it.

"Want me to get that?" Kendall asked.

"It's probably somebody I don't want to talk to."

"You should get call display."

"Never got around to it."

It rang once more and, shaking her head, Kendall reached to answer it.

"I'm not here," he told her as she picked up the receiver.

"Hello?"

Her voice was all crisp and businesslike, like a telephone operator. Then, instead of getting warmer, her tone crisped even more, like flash-frozen water. "Yes, he's here."

She handed him the phone.

"I said I didn't want to talk to anyone."

"It's Ashlee," she said.

"Oh." He took the phone. "Hey, Ash. What's up?"

"Harrison had to work and I'm bored," his ex-wife told him. Every word was a pout.

"Too bad." He didn't have a lot of sympathy. What did she expect, marrying a guy who got his jollies throwing family men out of work?

"Oh, Dy, what was I thinking?"

"Hell if I know. If you'd asked my opinion I'd have told you not to marry the guy."

He heard her sigh, long and dramatic. "I want him to be more like you."

"No, you do not. You are the classic grass-is-greener-on-the-other-side type. Ash, you divorced me. For good reasons." He was getting tired of these conversations, tired of terrific women who weren't getting what they needed from him because he didn't have whatever they were looking for in him to give.

"I know. When I'm with you, I want you to be more like Harrison."

A chuckle was surprised out of him. "If you're looking for sympathy, you came to the wrong guy."

"I'm not looking for sympathy. I'm looking for company. Harrison's gone to work, and I don't have anything to do."

Warning signs strobed across his brain. "I promised Kendall I'd show her my land today."

"Oh." She sounded deeply disappointed. "I've seen your land."

"Yeah. I know." Also, he hadn't invited her out here.

"Can you come for lunch?"

His immediate impulse was to say no, but he paused. "Is Harrison going to be there?"

"No. I told you. He has to work."

He should stay a long way away from Ashlee, but then Kendall was going to have lunch with his sister despite his obvious wishes to the contrary. Kendall also wasn't going to be around much longer to deflect Ashlee. Maybe it was time he told Ashlee once and for all that he was a man from her past, all right, and he'd be staying put in the past. He couldn't give any decent woman a future.

One evening with his own family had him realizing that Dy wasn't short for Dylan, it was short for dysfunctional.

He felt a little sorry for his ex-wife. She sure could pick 'em. Since he had a pretty good idea that having lunch with the man's wife would drive Harrison ballistic, he found one more reason to go.

"Sure. I'll drop Kendall off for her lunch date and then swing by your place. Around noon?"

"Doesn't matter. I'll be here all day, bored out of my mind."

"Are you making lunch?" If she was, he'd have to go out to eat first.

Ashlee giggled as if she'd read his mind. "I'm still the worst cook I know. I'll get Hettie to make something."

He got off the phone and found Kendall staring at him, bacon sizzling so loud it sounded as if it were having a temper tantrum. Kendall looked to be in a similar mood.

"Ashlee invited me for lunch at her house."

Kendall shook her head.

He made a desperate gesture. "What am I supposed to do?"

"Why don't you invite your mother to go along with you? She and Ashlee can try and patch the marriage back up. You'll make both their days."

He put on more coffee, trying not to notice how homey this was and how nice it was to have a woman around who liked to cook. She suited the place, he thought, watching Kendall. Even though she was irritated with him, she managed to move efficiently around the kitchen, cracking eggs and dropping them into the sizzling pan like a seasoned pro. He could manage scrambled eggs in the microwave, which was one meal more than Ash could cook. He doubted his mother even knew where the kitchen was.

Funny how you could miss something you'd never had.

The coffee was brewed and Kendall was deftly plating his breakfast when the phone rang again. "Maybe it's Harrison challenging you to a duel," his housemate said, sounding as if she'd dipped her voice in sugar.

Since she let the damn thing ring, he answered the phone.

"Hargreave," he snapped.

"Hargreave back at you," said the no-nonsense voice of Mary Beth on the other end. His sister was as emotionally stunted as he was, but at least she'd been smart enough not to marry.

"Hey, sis. What's up?"

"I'm stuck in court. There is no way I can get away for

lunch today. Unexpected problems. Can you tell Kendall?"

"Sure. You want to speak to her?"

"No. Don't have time. Ask her to leave a message at my office and we'll reschedule. I'm free tomorrow or Thursday."

"I'll tell her."

"Hey."

"What?"

"As weird as last night was, I liked seeing you again."

They weren't one of those touchy-feely families, and he knew she was saying a lot more than her words conveyed. "Me, too."

He thought she'd already hung up when she said, "I missed you."

"Me, too."

"Later." And she was gone.

He hung up slowly, thinking it was time he and Mary Beth started spending more time together. In spite of how screwed up the whole family dynamic was, he had a deep affection for his sister.

"What was that all about?"

"Mary Beth says she's sorry but she had to cancel lunch. Some legal thing got in the way."

"Okay. And you're smiling because…?"

"You just witnessed big-time family bonding."

"I'm overwhelmed with the emotion of the moment."

"Now, you're starting to sound like me."

Toast popped up from the toaster, and she deftly scooped two pieces and buttered them. "I am really happy that you and your sister realized how much you care about each other."

"You could see that? Really?"

"Yes. You didn't say a lot to each other, but you have a strong bond."

"I guess we do at that."

"Your parents, on the other hand…"

He snagged a piece of toast, crunched half of it and then waved the other half at her. "Don't say I didn't warn you," he said around the toast.

He called Ashlee. "Listen, Ash, Kendall's date canceled on her for lunch, so we're both coming."

He saw movement out of the corner of his eye. It was his breakfast chef waving her arms. A spatula she held in one hand looked as though it might do some damage.

"But…"

"Ashlee, she's my houseguest. I can't leave her home alone."

"Yes, you can," Kendall shouted so loud he had to put his hand over the mouthpiece before Ashlee heard her.

"I thought we could talk, the two of us."

"We can talk and this way we'll have a chaperone in case Harrison hears about it."

"Who cares what Harrison thinks?"

"He's your husband, Ash. You picked him. You should at least try and make this thing work."

He ended the call as soon as he could, then sat down, pleased with the way events were turning out, to enjoy his breakfast.

Kendall didn't look nearly as pleased. "Why did you say I'd go? I am not going to a very inappropriate lunch with your ex-wife."

"See, that's the brilliant thing. With you there, it won't be inappropriate."

"Grow up!" She banged his breakfast down so he could see the yolks of his eggs jiggle. Exactly how he liked them.

"You promised me," he said to her. "You promised. Two more weeks—that's all I'm asking."

She continued to glare at him. "Then what are you going to do, Dylan? Once I'm gone? Who's going to protect you from the big, bad ex-wife then?"

He glared right back at her. "There's stuff going on here you don't know anything about."

"Of course I know what's going on. It's a classic love triangle."

"I'm not in love with Ashlee," he yelled.

"Then why do you keep playing her games?"

"Can we drop this and eat?"

She sank into her chair and draped her napkin across her lap.

He dug in to eggs that were perfect, with the unmistakable smoky salt taste of bacon fat. The bacon was crisp, the way he liked it, a fact she must have filed away when he'd ordered in restaurants. He slathered more butter on his toast to mop up every last bite.

"Kendall," he said, "this is great."

"Thanks, but it's only bacon and eggs. Not too much of a culinary challenge."

She spooned up some of that no-fat fruit yogurt she liked so much. She'd sprinkled granola and fruit over top. She'd snuck some of the fruit onto his plate but he decided to look on it as decoration. He did manage to chug down the fresh-squeezed orange juice, though, just to show he wasn't completely opposed to healthy food.

He got to the end of the juice and said, "Yuck."

"You don't like orange juice? Everyone likes orange juice."

"I don't like it chewy. I like it better out of a box or a can."

"Philistine." She reached over and snagged a slice of bacon off his plate.

He grinned at her. "Can you really cook?"

She seemed surprised by the question, probably because he was eating food she'd cooked.

"Of course I can. I love cooking."

"Huh." He thought back. "I don't think I've ever been with a woman who cooks." He finished mopping up the last of the egg yolk with the last of the toast. "And that includes my mom."

"I only have a small galley kitchen in my apartment. In this gorgeous kitchen? I could work miracles."

"Honey, if you want to cook in my kitchen, I'd be more than happy to let you. Truth is, places to eat around here are pretty limited." He pushed his plate away and sipped coffee.

"Okay. I'll cook. I'm happy to do it." She leveled a crafty pair of gray eyes his way. "But if I'm cooking, I'll decide what we're eating."

"Are we talking health food here? 'Cause I gotta tell you, I can eat pizza every night before I'm eating an alfalfa sprout."

She sipped her coffee. "I see. What's your position on tofu?"

"Is that a motor oil? I'm not allowed to use it. Not one of my sponsors."

She rose and collected his plate. "It's going to be a very long two weeks."

As he watched her moving around his kitchen as naturally as if she belonged there, he thought two weeks was going to be all too short.

CHAPTER EIGHTEEN

THERE WERE a couple of trees that had come down. They'd been felled and bucked, and were ready to cut into firewood. After helping Kendall with the dishes, Dylan headed outside, grabbed an ax and started in.

For some reason, her comment about him playing Ashlee's games wouldn't leave him.

Considering Miss Stick-Her-Nose-In-Everything Kendall was supposed to be in love with him, she hadn't exactly gone all sweet and worshipful, like women usually did. Kendall in love with a man was a lot like Kendall not in love with a man, except for her being more pushy about giving him her opinions about his life.

Crack. He brought the ax down hard and made a nice split down the side of the log. Another couple of swings of the ax and he had four neat fire logs.

He pulled up another slice of tree and swung his ax again. He fell into a rhythm of work, feeling the impact of each blow of the ax along his arm and ricocheting down his spine.

Who did she think she was? A woman who got dumped by a guy named Marvin, and who managed to get herself demoted from the most boring job in the universe. Yep, she was a fine one to tell him how to run his life.

The sooner she was on her way, the better for everybody. Maybe he'd tell her he didn't need her for the next two weeks after all. She could pack her stuff up and go—today, if she wanted.

As the thought vanished, a kind of gnawing ache took its place. He didn't want her to go. She could say whatever she liked about luck not existing and statistics and analysis until they'd both gone deaf with old age, but the only thing he knew was that he was racing better than ever in his career. And yet it wasn't winning he thought about when she was around.

He thought about last night, and how she'd sided with him unequivocally when they dined with his parents. The idea of her as an exotic dancer or an actress was almost as funny as the way his folks had believed it.

She made him laugh and she made his life better and the thought of her leaving made him ache. Why was that?

He swung the ax hard. Why the hell was that?

He worked through until he figured it was time to clean up for lunch, stacked the wood and headed back into the kitchen. He went to wash up at the kitchen sink but Kendall pointed in the direction of the bathroom without saying a word.

Give the woman free rein in his kitchen and she started acting like a wife.

Although, he amended, not like the only wife he'd ever had. Ashlee had tried to cook a couple of meals, but mostly they'd eaten out or subsisted on takeout. Now that Ashlee had a cook and a housekeeper, Harrison wouldn't ever be subjected to her cooking. Of course, the way things were going, he wouldn't be subjected to Ashlee much longer, either.

Any more than Dylan was going to be subjected to Kendall.

ASHLEE AND HARRISON'S home was as grand inside as it was outside. The door was opened by a housekeeper, which for some reason irked Kendall. "If I had enough money to hire a housekeeper, I'd still answer my own door if I'd invited friends over," she whispered as they followed the middle-aged woman down the hall.

"That's why you'll never be a grand lady," Dylan told her.

"Fine by me."

"Fine by me, too."

She was insensibly pleased. "So, you mean you'd never hire a housekeeper?"

He shrugged. "Not live-in. I have someone come by whenever I'm coming home."

By this time they'd trailed through a home that could be confused with the set from the *Antiques Roadshow.*

"Ashlee likes antiques."

Kendall got the feeling that every antique store in Ashlee's path had been denuded of antebellum artifacts.

"And she gets what she wants?" Right now, Ashlee had her eye on Dylan, and Kendall wondered how long he was going to be able to escape his ex-wife's acquisitive grasp. The way she felt now, Kendall was thinking of marking him down to sweeten the deal.

It felt as if an arrow had pierced her chest when she thought of Dylan and Ashlee together again. They were never going to make each other happy, whatever Ashlee's astrologer thought. Kendall wanted to cling to

Dylan and make him promise that whatever he did, he wouldn't marry Ashlee again, but she bit her tongue. It wasn't her place to cling or demand. She had no right. Loving a man did not give her the right to make demands. She had a strong feeling that she was very, very good for him, but if he wanted to let her go, how could she stop him going back to a woman who was so obviously wrong for him?

Their feet echoed on the black-and-white marble floor tile and their reflection was bounced back from a multitude of mirrors, many wavy with age. Dark paintings of long-dead men and women dotted the walls. The furniture was period, the carpets soft with age. Then they came into the glassed-in conservatory where Ashlee sat in a wicker lounger flipping through *Glamour,* and it was like stepping into another age.

Ashlee looked soft and fragile, and even Kendall, who pretty much had her number, had to squelch an impulse to ask her if she needed a cup of tea.

Orchids were everywhere. Kendall had never seen so many. She knew they were notoriously difficult to grow, and these ones seemed to thrive. Not surprisingly, Ashlee seemed right at home among the difficult-to-tend hothouse flowers.

Looking at Ashlee was like looking in the window of the Versace store. She seemed too expensive, too unattainable, out of Kendall's budget altogether.

Dylan walked over and gave her a peck on the cheek, and Kendall was struck by the fact that he belonged in that world.

Kendall felt as if she should ask the housekeeper if she needed help in the kitchen.

"Hi, Kendall," her hostess said.

"Hi. I'm sorry Harrison isn't here," she said.

"If he's so worried about what I do all day and who I do it with, he should be here," Ashlee said in a burst of logic that Kendall had already discovered was peculiar to Ashlee.

Dylan, instead of answering, crossed the room to Kendall and rubbed her shoulders. "You cold, honey?"

Okay, so his logic was as peculiar as Ashlee's.

"No. I'm not cold."

"There's some champagne left from the wedding," Ashlee said, motioning to a wine cooler sitting on the wicker table, which, Kendall noted, was set for three. "Can you open it?"

Dylan glanced over at her and she shrugged. As clearly as if he'd spoken, Kendall knew that he was wondering about the propriety of drinking Ashlee and Harrison's wedding champagne. The way Kendall looked at it, it wasn't really their issue. If Ashlee was bound and determined to drive Harrison insane with jealousy, she seemed to be going about it the right way.

Dylan popped the cork of the Cristal and poured the wine into three flutes.

"Here's to us," Ashlee said, tilting her glass toward Dylan. He returned her toast, turned and repeated the gesture with Kendall, doing his best to include her.

She glanced at her watch and calculated how much of this she was going to have to put up with before they could leave.

Ashlee had put aside her magazine, but she wasn't knocking herself out as a hostess. Silence reigned.

"What beautiful orchids," Kendall said.

"Do you like them?" Ashlee asked.

"I think they're gorgeous. Do you grow them yourself?"

"You'll be sorry you asked," Dylan said with a groan.

"Oh, you are such a guy," Ashlee replied. For the first time, she looked at Kendall with real warmth. "I cultivate them. I swear I married Harrison for his conservatory. The orchids love it here. The light's perfect, the atmosphere is easy to control. He had a special misting system installed for me so I don't have to worry if we go away."

"So what's he planning to do at work today? More layoffs?"

She shrugged so that one of the lacy straps of her white silk camisole slipped off her shoulder. She didn't bother to hike it back up again. "I don't know what he does."

If ever Kendall had seen a bad case of buyer's remorse, this was it. If Ashlee could return her very valuable groom back to the store for a cash refund, she'd do it in an instant.

The housekeeper appeared with a tray of open-faced shrimp croissants. Dylan hated shrimp. Kendall knew it after only a few weeks with him, and Ashlee, who'd been married to the man, seemed to have forgotten, if she'd ever known. For some reason that small fact depressed Kendall. If she couldn't have Dylan, she at least wanted him to be happy.

During lunch, they talked about local people Kendall knew nothing about. At first, Dylan tried to bring Kendall into the conversation but after a while she could see him give up. It was too hard to get her up to speed on a lifetime of old friends. She felt, as she was certain Ashlee meant her to feel, like a stranger at an intimate family event.

She ate her croissant, and watched as Dylan scraped off the shrimp and ate only the bread, while Ashlee picked at the shrimp and nibbled only a corner of her croissant. They might as well have shared one sandwich.

"Coffee on the terrace, I think," Ashlee said to the housekeeper when she came to clear their plates.

Get in the car and go home, I think.

It was warm outside, but surprisingly pleasant on the veranda, overlooking the river and the big, old oaks. They sat in deep wicker armchairs with cherry-and-white striped cushions. Along with the coffee came a tray of fresh fruit and pecan tarts pretty enough to grace a magazine cover.

Dylan scarfed three. Kendall figured he was hungry from lunch.

They didn't talk about anything much, but Kendall was aware of an uncomfortable undercurrent of emotion. Ashlee wasn't only flirting with Dylan. It seemed there was a kind of desperation in her that made Kendall wonder what was really going on.

Perhaps she recognized the desperation to be loved because she felt it herself. She wondered which of them was the more pathetic and decided it was probably herself. At least Dylan had loved Ashlee once, or been close enough to it that he'd married her.

All Kendall had ever been was a counterfeit girlfriend—a roadblock to keep Ashlee from claiming him back. With her new self-knowledge, she saw how foolish she'd been to ever have agreed to play such a part. She'd fallen into Dylan's life so easily; no wonder he believed she could fall out of it as effortlessly.

And Dylan? What did he feel, she wondered, caught between two women? Looking at him, it was hard to believe he thought much of anything. He appeared to be the handsome, successful jock whose only concern was the next race.

While she was watching the golden couple, thinking how good Ashlee and Dylan looked together, Harrison came striding around the corner. He wore gray dress pants and a white short-sleeved shirt. He was looking grim, and his mouth firmed even more when he saw Dylan. Ashlee was leaning toward him and talking animatedly, and Kendall could imagine the scene from Harrison's eyes—the two former lovers chatting like the old friends they were, and Kendall sitting slightly apart, obviously left out of the tête-à-tête.

"Kendall, Hargreave," he said with a curt nod. "I didn't know you were entertaining, Ashlee. I'd have tried to come home earlier."

His wife fluttered her birdlike hands and said, "Well, I didn't plan to entertain, but I was bored when you left me here all alone, and I remembered I wanted to talk to Dylan about the hospital fundraiser."

Dylan blinked. "Since when are you interested in hospitals?"

She fiddled with a coffee spoon. "I need something to do with my time, is all."

"Ash has been volunteering in the children's ward," Harrison said with a note of pride. "She wants to get a big, new TV and some computer access for the older kids."

"That's great, Ash."

"Well, it's something I can do since I spend so much time alone," she said, glaring at Harrison.

"I hope everything's all right at work," Kendall said, thinking that Harrison wasn't upset merely about their visit.

"There was a malfunction on some equipment," he said shortly. "It means we won't run at full capacity for a couple of weeks until we can get it fixed." He rubbed a hand over his eyes. "The machinery's getting old and needs updating."

Kendall glared at Dylan, ready to jump in and talk over him if he tried to make any cracks about layoffs, but surprisingly, he didn't. Maybe it was as obvious to him as it was to her that Harrison wasn't happy about the situation.

Ashlee rose. "Do you want some lunch, honey?"

"No. Thanks."

"Or some champagne? I think there's some left."

He stared at his wife for a moment and said, "No. I'm going to go and check the new foal and then head back to work." So, he'd come home specially to spend time with his wife only to find her entertaining. Not good.

Ashlee smiled brightly. "Oh, what a good idea. Why don't you take Kendall with you? I'm sure she'd love to see a brand-new baby horse." Turning to Kendall she added, "Harrison owns a couple of racehorses. He bred one of the mares and she foaled two nights ago."

"Do you like horses, Kendall?"

"I don't know a lot about them, but I think they're beautiful."

"You'll love the baby," Ashlee said. "We call him Beau. Off you both go, and then I can talk Dylan into being part of my fundraising."

Harrison gazed steadily at Ashlee for a moment, and

Kendall felt her stomach knot. That woman was as subtle as a soap opera villainess. Then he turned to Kendall. "I'd be happy to show you if you're interested."

"Thank you," she said.

Dylan sent her a quick glance of appeal, but she decided he was big enough to fight off a woman who probably weighed a hundred pounds soaking wet.

If he wanted to fight her off.

CHAPTER NINETEEN

SHE SET OFF with Harrison down the sloping meadow toward the river.

"How do you like Wilkerton?"

"It's very nice. Peaceful."

He laughed shortly. "It wasn't very peaceful around Dylan when he was young. He was always one crazy hell-raiser."

"I can imagine."

The sun warmed her face and the industrious bees sounded like soft snoring. He led her down a path to a dusty, old red truck. "Oh," she said. "Can't we walk?"

"If you've got all day. It's pretty far. I use the truck most of the time."

"All right," she said and climbed in. They rode down a narrow gravel road that followed the river. Three big paddocks stood side by side and in the farthest one, a gorgeous black mare stood staring at them over the fence. Beside her stood a spindly-legged foal. "Oh, he's gorgeous," she said as they drew closer.

Harrison strode into an adjacent barn and emerged with a couple of apples. He let her feed the mare an apple while the foal nursed.

She enjoyed the feel of the sun on her face and the

smell of grass and horse. She tried not to think about what was going on on the veranda, but Harrison's thoughts were clearly bent in the same direction.

"So, I hear you met Dylan's parents."

"Yes." She kept staring ahead.

"He always lived for sports and he was crazy about engines. He was go-cart racing in grade school, and anybody could see he was good."

She smiled, imagining the little boy Dylan would have been. "I can imagine."

"Of course, his folks hated everything about it. They were always finding reasons to forbid him to go racing. If he didn't have straight *A*s, then he couldn't race until he did, stuff like that. It made him crazy and rebellious, and of course he got out of there the second he could."

"Why are you telling me this?"

He stared up at the deep blue sky, shoved his hands into his pockets. "I think you're a good person and can maybe help Dy. One day pretty soon, he's going to need someone like you standing by him."

A wave of sadness swamped her. "I'm leaving."

"Does he know that?"

She nodded, suddenly unable to speak.

"When?"

"Two weeks."

"Does he know you love him?"

"Yes." She thought of her declaration last night and Dylan's unsatisfactory response. "Yes, he knows."

"I'm sorry."

"Thanks."

They turned and walked back to the truck.

"How can he be so blind?" Harrison suddenly exploded.

"How can she?"

"I don't want to talk about Ashlee."

She didn't know what to say, so she kept her mouth shut and they drove back in silence. They parked the truck and returned to the house. The veranda was deserted, the cups and dessert cleared away.

"They're probably in the conservatory," Harrison said. "That's where Ash spends most of her time. She loves her orchids."

They entered the house and headed straight for the conservatory, where she stopped dead in the doorway.

If Kendall had wondered how she'd feel if Dylan ended up back in Ashlee's arms, she now had her answer.

She felt rotten.

Kendall and Harrison had walked in on Ashlee and Dylan kissing. Dylan was sitting in one of the deep wicker chairs with Ashlee perched on his lap, leaning over and kissing him passionately. Her hands were in his hair and her body tilted into his.

Dylan wasn't exactly throwing her to the ground. His hands were on her shoulders, not exactly yanking her in closer, but not throwing her off his lap, either.

Harrison cleared his throat in classic French farce fashion. Well, he was a character in a French farce—the outraged husband.

Ashlee jerked her head up and turned to face them. Her eyes were huge, her lips red and puffy. Dylan glanced straight at Kendall, but his expression was unreadable.

She doubted her expression was unreadable. She bet

she looked as miserable as she felt. Two weeks? He couldn't wait two lousy weeks?

There was one of those awful pauses when no one knows what to do or say. Ashlee didn't leap off Dylan's lap and Dylan, after a quick glance at Kendall, sent Harrison a want-to-solve-this-in-the-back-alley? glance.

"Well," said Harrison, walking slowly past Kendall and into the room. "I think this is what's called a compromising situation."

Ashlee's eyes glittered like a shopoholic on Fifth Avenue. It seemed she wasn't going to apologize or explain. It looked as though she was going to enjoy the show.

"I guess it is, at that," Dylan drawled back.

Since Kendall wasn't sure how she felt, apart from stunned that Dylan would do something so stupid, she had no urge to smooth over the awkward situation, which normally she'd be eager to do.

Maybe, just maybe, confrontation wasn't always a bad thing. And, from the red-hot vibes singeing the air, it seemed there was about to be one.

"Ashlee," Harrison said to his wife, in a remarkably calm tone, "would you like to step outside into the garden with me for a minute?"

The diminutive blonde seemed flummoxed that he spoke with so little drama. Her eyes darted to Kendall and then she rose off Dylan's lap—and not a moment too soon, in Kendall's opinion. She tossed her head in true spoiled-beauty style. "No," she said. "I would not. You'll only yell at me. And then you'll do something awful like beat up Dylan."

There was a derisive snort from the easy chair. "He can try."

"Well, anyway," Ashlee said, running a hand through her hair, "now that we're all here, we might as well discuss this like adults."

"Are you acting like an adult?" Harrison said to his wife. He sounded calm and more disappointed than irate. What was wrong with Ashlee that she couldn't see how much this man loved her?

It was clear to Kendall that Harrison was not acting the way Ashlee had expected him to. She blushed and fiddled with her rings. "I have…feelings for Dylan."

Dylan opened his mouth to speak, but Kendall shook her head at him. This scene, she felt certain, needed to be played out by Ashlee and Harrison.

Harrison walked closer to his wife, stopping about three feet away and sticking his hands into his pockets. "What I have to say to you, I'd have preferred to say in private. But if this is your choice, then maybe it's best."

She raised her eyes for a second and then dropped them back to her hands.

"I went into this marriage with a pretty good idea that you'd try to bail." He sent her a rueful look. "I didn't imagine it would be within the first few months, though."

"I'm sorry, I never meant—"

"Yes. You did. Maybe not consciously, but you chose marriage to me as easily as you'd choose your fall wardrobe. And you figured you could change me as easily, too."

Ashlee dropped her hands and stared at him. He had her full attention now.

"I'm telling you in front of God and Dylan and Kendall that this time, honey, you aren't getting out."

"What! What do you mean?"

"I'm not giving you a divorce."

"But I love Dylan!" she cried.

"You don't love anyone. I thought deep down you loved me, only you didn't want to admit to yourself that you could ever be happy with a respectable, Republican-voting, stable man who wants a family. No emotional fireworks, no wild living."

"I could never be the wife you want," Ashlee said.

"Cut the drama. I'm offering you a chance to give it a try. I'm done chasing you and I'm done playing the fool. Your place is with me. You vowed before God and two hundred family and friends that you'd be my wife. I think all of us were thinking you could stick to your word for a little longer."

"But my astrologer said my destiny was with a man from my past."

"In the first place, I think astrology is hogwash. In the second, I *am* a man from your past."

"But you don't love me." Her eyes were big and getting misty with emotion. Kendall wondered how she could keep up with the drama in her own life.

Harrison looked dumbfounded. "I married you."

"But you don't act like you love me. Dylan would never stand there talking at me if he'd caught me with another man."

"I'd like to think I'm a little more evolved than Dylan," he replied coolly. "No offense."

"None taken," said the man in the chair. Unlike

Kendall, whose stomach was in knots, Dylan seemed to be enjoying himself.

"Ashlee, this isn't about me, or Dylan. It's about you. Honey, I love you and I'm not going anywhere. Let me repeat myself, neither are you."

"But you caught me in another man's arms."

"I caught you in Dylan's arms and frankly, even if you'd been buck naked, we'd be having the same conversation." He stepped forward and took her hands in his.

"You're a drama princess. In training to be a drama queen. Frankly, I'm attracted to that in you. I can be a little analytical. I'm too serious. You add excitement to my life. But you, my darling, also need me."

"I don't," she whispered.

"You're scared. And when you're scared you do crazy things to drive people away. I've been in love with you since high school. I've seen your pattern. What you really want is someone who will stick. I'm telling you right now, I'm that man. I don't care what you do. Kiss the entire NASCAR roster, dance naked on the Internet. I'm not leaving you, and I'm not letting you leave me."

Ashlee hiccupped on a sob. "Don't you even care that I was kissing Dylan?"

"Of course I care. When we're done here I'm taking you upstairs to wash your mouth out with soap."

She backed swiftly away, pulling her hands back. "You can't. You wouldn't dare."

"I can and I will. Me and Dylan beating on each other would give you a thrill. Having your mouth washed out with soap will be unpleasant for you and a lot more satisfying for me."

"And you won't get your ass kicked, either," Dylan added helpfully.

"That's right," Harrison said with a gleam of humor. "I won't get my ass kicked, either."

"Why couldn't you just spank me like any normal man?"

"I know you. You'd like it too much."

For the first time since she'd known her, Kendall saw Ashlee look at her new husband with the same kind of expression she usually sent Dylan. "You'd do that?"

"I'm going to. I think you've been a spoiled brat for too long. I love you, and I guess maybe the only way you'll believe that is if I give you some of the tough love you should have had years ago."

"Dylan?" she shrieked, backing away. "You're not going to let my husband brutalize me—" she glanced furtively their way "—are you?"

"I do believe I am." Dylan rose, walked toward Harrison and held out a hand. "I think maybe I was wrong about you," he said.

They shook hands. Harrison said, "I appreciate that. Now I'm afraid I'm going to throw you out so I can deal with my wife."

Kendall was a feminist, of course. But she didn't stay to help fight off the advances of the brute husband even when Ashlee begged her to. If ever anyone had had it coming, this woman had.

"Kendall, you can't leave me. You're a woman. You've got to help me."

"Ashlee," Kendall said, feeling better than she'd felt all day, "I've got a mouth right here beside me that also needs washing out with soap."

She glanced at Dylan long enough to see a calculating expression cross his face. He might as well have said, "You and which army?" But she'd figure something out.

"Okay, then, bye," Harrison said, looking determined. He didn't call the housekeeper; he escorted them to the door himself, with such haste Kendall barely had time to turn and call through the doorway of the conservatory, "Thank you for lunch," before she was all but jogging down the marble halls toward the front door. Kendall didn't fool herself into thinking that Harrison had better manners than his wife. She knew he wanted to make sure they were off his property and that he had absolute privacy.

"WELL," DYLAN SAID once they'd returned to his house and as they started up the path to the kitchen door, "that was inter—"

He never got the rest of the word out. He gave a grunt as she launched herself at him, catching him with a headbutt to the stomach. Of course, if he'd seen her coming he'd have fought her off, but she caught him by surprise and she knocked him off balance. He tripped and she followed, shoving at him until they both fell in the dirt.

"What are you doing?"

She lay sprawled on top of him. "How could you be so stupid?" she shrieked.

"I couldn't stop her."

"Oh, right. Because she's so much bigger and stronger than you are? What did she do? Hold you down?" She was yelling right into his face and it felt good. Great, in fact. She wasn't a confrontational person, or a violent one, but something red-hot had snapped inside her and needed venting. She hauled back and whacked him in the chest with her fist. Then she did it again.

"Ow. Would you quit that?"

"She is married." Whack. "To another man." Whack. "She doesn't love you."

Vainly he tried to catch her swinging arm, but she was too quick for him. "Would you stop whaling on me and listen?" he yelled back.

"No." Whack. "I'm doing the talking." Whack.

"Yelling."

"You deserve it."

Suddenly, the world tilted and she found herself flipped on her back with Dylan on top of her. Even as she formed her hands back into fists, he grabbed them, one in each hand, and pulled her arms over her head.

"Bully," she said, glaring up at him.

"You were the one beating up on me," he reminded her, looking down at her with his eyes crinkling. They were chest-to-chest, belly-to-belly, thigh-to-thigh. Even though he was heavy and half squishing her, she was aware of her heart pounding, of the smell of him and of earth and moss-scented air, of the sky above where a few clouds floated dreamily.

His gaze intensified and she watched his mouth come toward hers. She jerked her head to the side. "I know where that mouth has been," she snapped.

"What was I supposed to do? Throw the woman on the floor?"

"Seems like a good idea."

"You abandoned me."

"I'm not always going to be around to protect you.

Maybe you need to figure out how to keep that woman's tongue out of your mouth all on your own. You know she wants you back."

"Well, she's not getting me back." He chuckled. "I think Harrison's going to see to that. Maybe he's not so much of a dork as I thought."

"Maybe." She tried to wriggle out from under him, but it was hopeless. "Can I get up now?"

"Are you going to hit me again?"

"Not unless you make me mad."

He still didn't move. His gaze narrowed. "What about the other thing? Am I going to spend all day dodging you and bars of soap while you try to wash my mouth out?"

"You could stay still and take your punishment like a man," she suggested, rather reasonably, she thought.

"Not going to happen. I had my mouth washed out once by my mom after I cussed. I still remember it."

She put her head back so she could look up at the trees and sky. In truth, she was enjoying this and wasn't in a big hurry for it to end.

"Well," she said, "you have to consider my position. I said I was going to wash your mouth out with soap. I'm a woman who follows through. It's one of my better qualities."

"I can see your problem," he said, shifting slightly so his chest rubbed hers through her dress. "How 'bout we compromise?"

"I believe in compromise," she agreed, liking the way the sun made a halo of his hair and the way he was looking at her, deep into her eyes. "What did you have in mind?"

He switched her wrists to his left hand and with his

right, nudged her hair behind her ear and trailed his fingers from her shoulder to her earlobe.

His voice was soft and slow, like thick, rich honey. "You sure do have some of the softest skin I've ever felt."

She sighed when his lips followed the path of his fingers. "Toothpaste," he said softly.

"Toothpaste?" She jerked her eyes all the way open and tried to concentrate. What on earth would they do with toothpaste?

He was smiling down at her now in a very disconcerting way, obviously reading her confused thoughts. "To wash out my mouth. Would you consider toothpaste? Instead of soap?"

It would be so much easier to think if he'd stop stroking her in that slow, deliberate way. Still, she tried to hold on to her concentration. "Let me get this straight," she said, losing part of the last word in a sigh of pleasure as his lips tugged on her earlobe. "You want to substitute having your mouth washed out with soap with—brushing your teeth?"

He appeared to think about this deeply. "I want to be absolutely fair about this. I guess you could brush them for me."

She was too far gone down the path of loving him, and he was too ridiculous. "Oh, Dylan," she said.

Love is such a gift, she thought as she stared up at him, hers to give. Even though he didn't love her back, she was the better for loving him. Of that she was certain.

"Come on." He rose gracefully and helped her to her feet. "Let's go wash my mouth out."

She brushed at the collection of dirt and leaves and

twigs that decorated her dress, then followed him inside, all the way to his bedroom where, even though there was no one but them in the house, they shut the door behind them.

CHAPTER TWENTY

THE SWARM of the pit crew buzzed around Kendall in ordered chaos as the team made the final preparation for today's race at Indianapolis. Dylan had signed his last prerace autograph, given his final interview, and he only had one job left to do before climbing into his vehicle.

This was the moment she'd come to treasure. There wasn't a lot of media today; one camera and a single print journalist. A dozen people who'd somehow wangled garage passes and the crew were on hand for the ritual.

Dylan wore his usual charm like armor, preventing anyone from getting too close. Still, she responded as she always did to the warm light in his eyes, to the half serious, half playful way he walked up to her.

"Good luck, Dylan," she said, hanging on to her smile even though her heart felt as if it were imploding. For she knew what he didn't yet—this would be their last kiss.

After the wonderful night they'd spent together, she knew she had to get out while she still could.

She hoped her words would echo in his mind when he realized she was gone, and that he'd understand she'd meant it as a goodbye. She did wish him luck. She wished him everything in life that he deserved and didn't understand he even wanted. Family, children, a future that extended farther than the next race.

He held her shoulders for a moment, looking down into her face, almost as if he knew. And then he dipped his head. She closed her eyes and felt the warm impact as his lips covered hers.

Usually, their prerace kisses were brief, but as she felt the pressure lessen as he started to pull away, it was as though he couldn't break the connection, not yet. Suddenly he was pulling her hard against him. She made a little sound of pleasure and protest, and *oh, yes, please,* and then she threw her arms around his neck and kissed him for all she was worth. It was a kiss to keep in her memory forever, a kiss to bring out and treasure when she was lonely and wishing things could have been different. That he could have been strong enough to overcome his demons and fight for her. For them.

When he lifted his head, his palm cupped her cheek for one more moment of painful intimacy. "Don't go anywhere," he said.

She didn't reply, because she was an honest person, so she took the helmet from his crew chief and slipped it onto his head.

Dylan pulled out and took his place on the track. Her adrenaline began to pump.

When the race started, the roar was like a hundred jets, and the cars flew past at speeds that still astonished her and seemed more like flight than any earthbound travel.

After being a NASCAR good-luck charm, she'd come to feel part of this amazing spectacle. She knew those guys currently flying around the track, knew their wives and families. Part of her wanted them all to win, but in her heart of hearts, she'd give Dylan a tiny head start.

She shaded her eyes against the sun, watched and sent her good-luck vibes Dylan's way.

This was how she wanted to remember him.

There would be no goodbye, because she couldn't get through goodbye without making a fool of herself and she was done making a fool of herself over men.

The woman who once would have settled for Marvin Fulford as a life partner now knew her own worth. She'd never settle again. Not for a man who didn't truly love her, even if that man was Dylan Hargreave, the man who would always own a part of her heart.

If she tried to say goodbye, he was going to talk her out of leaving. He'd use his charm and warmth and the fact that she loved him to convince her to stay for the rest of the season. He'd ask her to stay for the team, and she was crazy enough that she might agree.

Except that Kendall was tired of being a team player. Once, just once, she wanted to be the star of the show, the person other people put themselves out to impress or help. She'd brought Dylan good luck and for that she was happy. Actually, she believed he'd gained confidence from believing she brought him luck. But whatever the reason, his team had been racing so much better since she'd been around. She had to accept that good luck for Dylan was bad luck for her.

Nothing but more pain could result if she hung around accepting public kisses and private loving that meant the world to her and so little to him. They hadn't spoken again about the two weeks' notice, but when he got her letter, he'd understand.

So she watched, choosing not to be hooked in by the headset so she could overhear Dylan talking to his team. Right now, she only wanted to watch as his car stayed glued to the rest of the pack. She knew now it was called riding the draft, using the aerodynamics of the cars in front to suck him forward.

She waited as long as she could. Dylan made his final pit stop and there was maybe an hour to go in the race.

When she climbed down off the hauler, no one noticed, or if they did would think she was going to the restroom or to take a walk.

DYLAN'S WORLD telescoped into the track ahead. Heat, dust, noise, some kind of rattling he didn't like the sound of and hoped would go away if he ignored it. Thirty laps to go. Come on. Hang in there, he silently ordered.

"Something's going on," he told his crew chief a few minutes later. "Something's rattling and it feels like the back end's loose."

"Fifteen laps. Take her easy."

"Yeah."

He was holding his position, but it was all he could do. There'd be no screaming to victory today. All he could hope for was a top-ten finish and that he didn't stop dead in the middle of the track with only a few laps to go.

"Come on, sweetheart," he said softly, knowing that Kendall was out there watching, his superserious darling of a good-luck charm. Thinking about her made him relax a little. There wasn't anything he could do, anyway. When the race was over and he was all cleaned up, he'd take her out somewhere nice. Only the two of them, and see if he could charm her out of her truly terrible notion of leaving.

Now that they'd become intimate, how could she even think of going? She wasn't a quitter. He'd make her see that leaving now would put not only him but the whole team in a bad position. She wasn't the kind of woman to let people she cared about down. And she did care about him.

A prickle of discomfort brushed his spine. She cared about him a lot. He knew that. Truth was, he cared about her, too, but he wasn't a settling-down man. By now she must be able to see that.

Who'd want a guy with a messed-up background like his anyhow? A man who was going around in circles like the cars on this track? This was the only thing he was really good at. Couldn't she see that? He'd suck at being a family man.

He needed to see her, though. The laps couldn't roar by fast enough. In spite of the ominous rattle and the excellent advice to take it easy, he didn't take it easy. He pushed it, reaching for a little more speed. A little more juice. Enough to get to Kendall before she did anything crazy.

And then more luck showered down on him. Bad luck, to be sure, but bad luck directed at another driver. The very thing he'd dreaded happening to him instead got somebody else. He passed one poor sucker who'd run out of gas. It happened. And two stock cars that had been too close to pull back got caught, too.

And Dylan found himself rattling all the way to the finish line, landing himself a fourth-place finish.

Not bad, he thought with a grin.

Not bad at all.

He hauled himself out and blinked, momentarily unsteady on his feet. He had a strange moment of dizziness and blinked again. Maybe his eyes were cloudy from fatigue but he had an instant's vision of Kendall running toward him, like in a movie clip, so even as he saw her he knew she wasn't real, even though he felt himself running toward her as in a dream. There were three kids running behind her, and he knew in his gut they were his kids. His and Kendall's. He had never felt such joy in his life as he did in that moment. His sight cleared almost immediately and he found himself wishing the vision had remained a little longer—so he could get closer to his family. However, though the noise and crowds and the post-race craziness started up again around him, his sense of certainty remained. Kendall wasn't just his lucky charm—she was his destiny.

He sprinted toward his crew, his gaze sweeping the area looking for the woman he'd so nearly lost. Where was she? Urgency gripped him when he didn't immediately spot her.

"Nice going, Dy," Mike said.

"Thanks. Where's Kendall?" he yelled.

His crew chief gazed around. "I don't know. She was here before."

He jogged through the craziness, but he didn't see her. He checked with the closest security guard, who said, "Dylan. That nice young gal you keep kissing left this for you."

An awful coldness settled in his gut.

He took the envelope and said, "Thanks," but he felt no gratitude. His name in Kendall's neat handwriting filled him with dread. She'd even sealed the envelope.

Premeditated was what he thought as he ripped it open and pulled out a one-page letter. She'd planned on leaving. Because he knew, the minute he saw the letter, that she was already gone.

"How long ago did she give you this?" he asked, having read through the message.

"'Bout an hour ago."

"Good race, Dy."

"Thanks, Carl. You, too," Dylan said, belatedly remembering that Carl Edwards had come in ahead of him in the number-three spot.

"Everything okay?"

Edwards might be a good ol' boy lady charmer, but he was also a friend. And right now, with the way Dylan felt, as if somebody'd taken a tire iron to his knees, he could use a friend.

Unable to explain, he handed over Kendall's letter. Carl glanced at it and read aloud.

"Dear Dylan.

"I've left. I'm sorry. I couldn't stay and say goodbye properly. It would have been too hard, and I suspect you are a man who hates weeping females."

Carl glanced up and said, "Show me a guy who doesn't."

"Read the rest of it." Maybe if he heard it aloud he could take in the message.

"I had so much fun being with you and the team for the last few months. I'll never forget my NASCAR initiation. I didn't bring you luck, Dylan. You had it all along.

"Please say goodbye to everyone for me.

"I'll miss you all.

"Drive carefully,

"Kendall."

Carl passed the letter back, with a look on his face that suggested he didn't have a clue what to say.

"What kind of way is that to say goodbye?" Dylan sputtered, suddenly angry. "She doesn't even end the letter properly. No *sincerely,* no *regards,* no *love, Kendall.*"

"She didn't need to say it, Dy. The love is all over that note."

Dylan snorted. "Where?"

"See this part here? Where the paper got wet?" He pointed to a splotch on the white page that Dylan hadn't noticed.

"Yeah."

"She was crying."

"You think?"

"Like a baby."

He blew out a breath. "Then why didn't she stay?"

"You know why. And if you don't, go down and ask any driver here. Even better, ask their wives or girlfriends. She loves you, Dy. And she isn't the kind of woman to hang around if you don't love her back."

Dylan snatched the letter, which was getting grimy since neither of them had showered yet. "I'm taking dating advice from a guy who guest-starred on a soap opera."

Carl laughed. He was obviously not a man who was torn apart by a woman who wanted more than he had to offer. "I'm still trying to figure out women. But since you asked, here's what you gotta do. Figure out what is stopping you from falling on your knees and begging that great girl to marry you."

"I can't—"

"And when you figure it out, you fall on your knees and you ask her, real nice."

"But—"

"'Cause if you don't, there's plenty of men around who could use your luck."

He wasn't talking about racing luck, and they both knew it.

Dylan replaced the letter in the envelope. "I messed up, didn't I?"

"Big-time."

And with a slap on the back, Edwards walked on.

He'd messed up bad.

CHAPTER TWENTY-ONE

HE TRIED to think, but he felt unfamiliar panic swamp his brain. He could remain cool under some pretty hairy stuff, but he'd never faced losing everything before. And that, he realized with a zing, was what he was facing.

Kendall was the person who made sense of it all. She was right, of course. She hadn't brought him luck. She'd brought him the missing part of himself, the part that had been frozen out, ignored and punished by his family, so he'd ceased to believe his love was worth anything to anyone.

There'd been no conditions to Kendall's love. She didn't care if he was perfect, didn't expect it of him. She'd given him the most amazing gift and he'd tried to give it back. Pretended it meant nothing. He now realized that it did. The gift of her love meant everything to him. All that she asked of him was that he look into his own heart and see what she saw so clearly, that they were a matched pair. Salt and pepper, love and laughter, his car and a racetrack.

Now, he had to convince her of that.

He didn't bother to change. No time. He was hot, tired and sweat-stained, but there was no time. No time. No time. It beat like a chant in his head.

He jogged back to his crew chief, who was looking at him with concern. "Everything okay, there, Dylan?"

"No. Everything's terrible. Kendall's gone."

"Don't panic. She's probably gone back to the trailer."

"No. I screwed up. No time to explain. I need to get to the airport."

Mike shook his head. "The traffic will be insane getting out of here."

"I know," he said. "I need the company's chopper right now to get me to the airport."

"Okay. Take it easy. I'll set it up. Why don't you go shower and clean up?"

"No time." He couldn't explain the sense of urgency that hung over him, but he didn't even try. Kendall was leaving and he had to stop her.

"I need to find out when the next plane to Portland leaves."

KENDALL COULDN'T explain the sense of urgency that hung over her. She needed to get away. Impossible to understand. She urged the cab driver to go faster, not that it was going to make the plane leave any sooner, but being at the airport was going to help her a great deal.

She was being ridiculous, she knew. She had at least an hour's start on Dylan. Then there'd be all that media stuff to deal with, and the fans. He wouldn't even get her letter until he left the security entrance. Then, if he tried to follow her, the traffic would be a killer. She'd be gone before he had a chance to stop her. *If* he wanted to stop her, and why would he?

She breathed a sigh of relief when the cab dropped her off at the airport.

Of course he wasn't following her. How egotistical of her to even consider the possibility. So she hadn't reminded him that his two weeks were up. He knew the score.

Her heart—no, make that her gut, that intuitive center that she'd only started listening to—was throwing a great, huge hissy. Don't go back to your old life, it said. But what else could she do?

A nanosecond's thought answered that question. What should she do? She should say no to their oh-so-flattering sideways promotion. What had she been thinking?

There were other companies, other jobs, and perhaps it was time for her to move on.

She was relatively young, definitely single, unattached; she could work anywhere. If life with NASCAR had taught her anything, it was that victory goes to the bold.

Maybe it was time for the most cautious woman in the United States to take a chance, to embrace risk.

She was smiling, seeing herself in a new life that had nothing to do with her old company, when she heard her name being called. Not only her ears perked up when she heard her name, but every cell in her body jumped to vital, living attention.

It was him.

Impossibly, ridiculously, against the odds of traffic, timing, her careful planning, Dylan was here.

"Kendall!"

Dylan bounded toward her as though he'd this second jumped out of his car.

"You didn't change," she said stupidly.

"No time," he panted, and she realized he'd run a long way.

"Where did you come from?"

"Helicopter."

She groaned. How had she thought she could beat him at any kind of a racing thing?

He walked to her and her heart jumped. Something about him was different. It took her a minute to realize it was the expression on his face and in his eyes when he looked at her.

"Don't go," he said.

"I have to."

"No. You don't."

He sat beside her in the departure lounge—and how on earth had he got through security, anyway? she thought with annoyance.

He took her hand. It was warm. A little gritty.

"There's something I need to ask you before you go."

"Is it about the luck thing?"

"No."

"Oh."

"Are you done guessing? Can I ask my question now?"

She shrugged. "I guess."

"Kendall." He took the other hand, as well, so he clasped both her hands against his chest.

"Yes?"

"Would you marry me?"

She looked at him for a moment. "That's it?"

"Don't you want to?"

"I feel like you're trying to race the last lap without putting in all the laps that come before it."

He nodded. "Sorry. I'm a little nervous."

She wouldn't smile, she mustn't smile, otherwise he'd think she was weak and easy. But she wanted to smile so badly. Dylan Hargreave nervous? In front of her?

Life was sweet.

Her heart was hammering as though it would break through the wall of her chest, but she wouldn't make this easy for him. She'd been too easy before. Now it was time for both of them to see how special she was.

He took a deep breath. "I don't believe in luck, either."

"You don't?"

"No. I think you're right. When I started kissing you and making you a big part of my life, and then I started winning, I figured it was a totally random thing. Luck."

She nodded.

"But it wasn't luck. You make me feel better about myself, you make me race better—"

"That's not a good enough—"

"Of course it's not a good enough reason to marry a person and I'm disappointed you would even think that of me. The point is that everything about you makes me feel better. I'm better in every area of my life when you're around. I work better, sleep better, feel better. I'm happier. I'm not the brightest guy in the world sometimes and I can't believe how long it took me to figure this out, but I love you."

He looked at her so hopefully. "I want to believe you," she said.

"Then do. Believe that you are a fantastic woman and I'm an idiot for not seeing sooner that you are the other part of myself. The missing piece."

"How can you have suddenly changed your mind?"

she asked him. "When I told you I loved you, you looked sort of embarrassed."

"It was the craziest thing that's ever happened to me. I got out of my car at the end of the race and I had this sort of—I don't know. It sounds stupid, but it was a vision. Gray and blurry at first, but then absolutely clear. You were running toward me, and I was running for you." His voice grew husky as he relived those moments. She felt the intensity of his experience in the tension in his body.

"As I got closer you know what I saw?"

She didn't say a word, only shook her head.

"Our kids."

She blinked, looking startled. "Our kids?"

He nodded. A smile blooming. "Know how many there were?"

She didn't say a word. Only shook her head again.

"Three. Three of 'em. And they were running toward me from behind you. And you know what?"

She shook her head again.

"I wasn't scared or freaking. It felt right. So right." He blinked, and only then did she see the wetness on his cheek. "Kendall, I love you. I love our three kids who aren't even born yet. And I love that we can have a great life together. Please, please marry me."

She looked at him, at the man she loved to the depth of her being, and wondered about luck and chance and fate, all the forces that had brought them together. "I thought it wasn't going to work out. That you would never figure out that we are so right together. I thought I'd be brave and go start a new life." She sniffed, trying to hold her emotions together. "But all I wanted was to be back at the track with you."

"We're going to start our new life together," he promised, "if you say yes."

She nodded, a smile of pure joy flooding her face. "Oh, yes. I'll marry you."

He pulled her against him and they stayed there, while passengers came and went and more than a few curious stares were lobbed their way. "Three, huh?"

"A boy, a girl and a little one that I didn't get a good look at."

Her smile grew misty. "It's nice to know there are some surprises still ahead of us."

* * * * *

Happily ever after is just the beginning...

Turn the page for a sneak preview of
A HEARTBEAT AWAY
by
Eleanor Jones

Harlequin Everlasting—Every great love
has a story to tell. ™
A brand-new series from Harlequin Books.

Special? A prickle ran down my neck and my heart started to beat in my ears. Was today really special?

"Tuck in," he ordered.

I turned my attention to the feast that he had spread out on the ground. Thick, home-cooked-ham sandwiches, sausage rolls fresh from the oven and a huge variety of mouthwatering scones and pastries. Hunger pangs took over, and I closed my eyes and bit into soft homemade bread.

When we were finally finished, I lay back against the bluebells with a groan, clutching my stomach.

Daniel laughed. "Your eyes are bigger than your stomach," he told me.

I leaned across to deliver a punch to his arm, but he rolled away, and when my fist met fresh air I collapsed in a fit of giggles before relaxing on my back and staring up into the flawless blue sky. We lay like that for quite a while, Daniel and I, side by side in companionable silence, until he stretched out his hand in an arc that encompassed the whole area.

"Don't you think that this is the most beautiful place in the entire world?"

His voice held a passion that echoed my own

feelings, and I rose onto my elbow and picked a buttercup to hide the emotion that clogged my throat.

"Roll over onto your back," I urged, prodding him with my forefinger. He obliged with a broad grin, and I reached across to place the yellow flower beneath his chin.

"Now, let us see if you like butter."

When a yellow light shone on the tanned skin below his jaw, I laughed.

"There…you do."

For an instant our eyes met, and I had the strangest sense that I was drowning in those honey-brown depths. The scent of bluebells engulfed me. A roaring filled my ears, and then, unexpectedly, in one smooth movement Daniel rolled me onto my back and plucked a buttercup of his own.

"And do *you* like butter, Lucy McTavish?" he asked. When he placed the flower against my skin, time stood still.

His long lean body was suspended over mine, pinning me against the grass. Daniel…dear, comfortable, familiar Daniel was suddenly bringing out in me the strangest sensations.

"Do you, Lucy McTavish?" he asked again, his voice low and vibrant.

My eyes flickered toward his, the whisper of a sigh escaped my lips and although a strange lethargy had crept into my limbs, I somehow felt as if all my nerve endings were on fire. He felt it, too—I could see it in his warm brown eyes. And when he lowered his face to mine, it seemed to me the most natural thing in the world.

None of the kisses I had ever experienced could have even begun to prepare me for the feel of Daniel's lips on mine. My entire body floated on a tide of ecstasy that shut out everything but his soft, warm mouth, and I knew that this was what I had been waiting for the whole of my life.

"Oh, Lucy." He pulled away to look into my eyes. "Why haven't we done this before?"

Holding his gaze, I gently touched his cheek, then I curled my fingers through the short thick hair at the base of his skull, overwhelmed by the longing to drown again in the sensations that flooded our bodies. And when his long tanned fingers crept across my tingling skin, I knew I could deny him nothing.

* * * * *

Be sure to look for A HEARTBEAT AWAY, available February 27, 2007.

And look, too, for
THE DEPTH OF LOVE
by Margot Early,
the story of a couple who must learn that love
comes in many guises—and in the end
it's the only thing that counts.

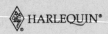

REQUEST YOUR FREE BOOKS!
2 FREE NOVELS PLUS 2 FREE GIFTS!

SPECIAL EDITION®
Life, Love and Family!

YES! Please send me 2 FREE Silhouette Special Edition® novels and my 2 FREE gifts. After receiving them, if I don't wish to receive any more books, I can return the shipping statement marked "cancel." If I don't cancel, I will receive 6 brand-new novels every month and be billed just $4.24 per book in the U.S., or $4.99 per book in Canada, plus 25¢ shipping and handling per book and applicable taxes, if any*. That's a savings of at least 15% off the cover price! I understand that accepting the 2 free books and gifts places me under no obligation to buy anything. I can always return a shipment and cancel at any time. Even if I never buy another book from Silhouette, the two free books and gifts are mine to keep forever.   235 SDN EEYU 335 SDN EEY6

Name	(PLEASE PRINT)	
Address		Apt.
City	State/Prov.	Zip/Postal Code

Signature (if under 18, a parent or guardian must sign)

Mail to the **Silhouette Reader Service™:**
IN U.S.A.: P.O. Box 1867, Buffalo, NY 14240-1867
IN CANADA: P.O. Box 609, Fort Erie, Ontario L2A 5X3

Not valid to current Silhouette Special Edition subscribers.

Want to try two free books from another line?
Call 1-800-873-8635 or visit www.morefreebooks.com.

* Terms and prices subject to change without notice. NY residents add applicable sales tax. Canadian residents will be charged applicable provincial taxes and GST. This offer is limited to one order per household. All orders subject to approval. Credit or debit balances in a customer's account(s) may be offset by any other outstanding balance owed by or to the customer. Please allow 4 to 6 weeks for delivery.

Your Privacy: Silhouette is committed to protecting your privacy. Our Privacy Policy is available online at www.eHarlequin.com or upon request from the Reader Service. From time to time we make our lists of customers available to reputable firms who may have a product or service of interest to you. If you would prefer we not share your name and address, please check here. ☐

Hearts racing
Blood pumping
Pulses accelerating

Falling in love can be a blur…especially at

180 mph!

So if you crave the thrill of the chase—on and off the track—you'll love

SPEED BUMPS
by **Ken Casper!**

On sale May 2007

www.GetYourHeartRacing.com

Hearts racing
Blood pumping
Pulses accelerating

Falling in love can be a blur...especially at
180 mph!

So if you crave the thrill of the chase—on and off the track—you'll love

SPEED BUMPS
by Ken Casper!

On sale May 2007

www.GetYourHeartRacing.com